# Gun Play at Convict Lake

This is the Saga of the Historical 1871 Nevada State Prison Break as Six of the Twenty-nine Escapees Fled South. After Killing a Mail Rider Near Sweetwater, Nevada, They Travelled on into California's Eastern Sierra Nevada Where Their Atrocities Continued.

Hearing of Their Deeds, a Posse from Benton Hot Springs Followed the Six Desperados to Beautiful Monte Diablo Lake Above Long Valley. A Murderous Gun Battle Took Place September 23, 1871.

Not Long After the Shoot Out, Local Mono and Inyo County Residents Renamed the Site Where Robert Morrison and Mono Jim Were Killed - Convict Lake.

Written by Richard Delaney
Illustrated by Debora Delaney

# Gun Play
## at
## Convict Lake

Written by Richard Delaney
Illustrated by Debora Delaney
Cover Design and Graphics by Talahi Media Arts
Printed and Distributed by Talahi Publishing
Talahi.com
P.O. Box 360, Prather, CA 93651

Copyright 2008

ISBN-9706798-3-3-1

# Forward

*Gun Play at Convict Lake* is the story of the events following the escape of six of the 29 felons from the Nevada State Prison in September 1871. It chronicles their specific activities and details the fate that awaited them. It is based on actual newspaper accounts spanning a period of approximately four years. Few actual pictures of the participants exist. Therefore, the personal photographs in the book are based on the "Pen Portrait" descriptions written by the journalists of the era. Other pictures were created for the book to help depict the actions described. The events noted herein are based upon accounts given by the participants as noted in the periodicals of the time.

In developing the story, a thorough search was made of the Nevada State Prison records, a variety of documented newspaper reports of the time, Nevada State Library Historical Archives, Nevada State Museum and the Nevada Historical Society at the University of Nevada, Reno. Other sources included the Mono County Museum, Bridgeport, CA; Mono County Historical Society, Bridgeport, CA; the Eastern Sierra Museum in Independence, CA; and the Laws Railroad Museum in Bishop, CA.

The author would like to thank the following for their contributions toward making this story as factual as possible. Kent Stoddard, Mono County Historical Society; Terri Gessinger, Bodie State Historic Park Historian; Kathy Edwards, Research Librarian, Nevada State Library Archives; Jeff Kintop, State Archives Manager, Department of Cultural Affairs, Nevada State Library and Archive; Robert Nylen, Curator of History, Nevada State Museum; Tim Purdy, Lassen County Calif. Historian and Erin Delaney, Proofreader.

# Table of Contents

| | |
|---|---|
| Desperate Men Make Desperate Plans | 2 |
| All Hell Breaks Loose | 10 |
| A Trek Through the Pine Nut Mountains | 19 |
| The Unfortunate Billy Poor | 27 |
| Searching for the Jones' Gang | 38 |
| Stopping Over at The McLaughlin Ranch | 46 |
| Benton Hot Springs Posse Hits the Trail | 52 |
| The Deadly Shootout at Monte Diablo | 57 |
| Morrison Buried - Morton and Black Hung | 66 |
| Roberts, Burke and Cockerell Back in Jail | 68 |
| Whatever Happened to Charlie? | 70 |
| Epilogue | 72 |
| Map of the Jones' Gang Journey | 73 |

# Gun Play at Convict Lake

Early Carson City, Nevada

Abe Curry's Warm Springs Hotel

The Nevada State Prison

# Gun Play at Convict Lake

## Desperate Men Make a Desperate Plan

The Nevada State Prison in Carson City was the residence of a cadre of unsavory characters in 1871. Nearly 70 men were serving sentences ranging from murder to train robbery to arson, rape, assault and burglary. These were not nice men. To no one's surprise, they didn't want to be there. The talk of escape was constantly on their lips. On September 3, several of the more desperate figured it was time for a break. All they needed was a plan.

Leandor Morton and Frank Clifford were selected to plan the escape. Morton was in jail for train robbery back in December. He was suspected in the deaths of two U.S. Cavalry soldiers, whose bodies were never found. When arrested Lea was wearing the gloves of one of those men. He was lucky not to have been charged with murder as well. Morton asked that Frank Clifford work with him. Early on Clifford had chosen a life of crime. He frequently ended up in jail. But, he never stayed long. He was considered to be one of the best escape artists on the west coast. Lea thought him a natural to help plan the escape. The reason Clifford was in prison this time was for stage robbery.

The basis of their plan was gaining access to the prison roof. To reach the roof, they would cut a hole in the ceiling above their jail cells. This had to be done so no trace of the work would be noticed by the guards during periodic checks. Once in the ceiling, part of the wall would also be dug out to get access to the roof. From there, they would break through to the second floor of the prison which housed the Warden's family, the Assistant Warden, an office and the armory. After dropping into the room below, they would break open the armory. With weapons in hand, they would fight their way downstairs, out into the yard and through the main gate. At that point, they would simply overpower any remaining guards and head for the Carson River.

Work began a week later. By Sunday the 17, preparations

## Gun Play at Convict Lake

were complete. That morning, as usual, the nearly 70 prisoners were taken to the dining hall for their breakfast. They knew the routine. They will stay all day. Some will play cards or checkers. Others will talk about old and better times. Word was spread amongst select prisoners that 6 pm was the time for action. A signal was to be given by Pat Hurley. He was to rattle his leg chains and drop his iron ball to the floor. Those that knew what was coming tried to remain as calm as possible. They tried to nonchalantly eat their evening meal, but the adrenaline was flowing.

Two hundred miles to the south, just outside Benton Hot Springs in Mono County, California, Robert Morrison and his fiancé, Sarah Devine shared a kiss. The late fall afternoon was quickly cooling off. The two lovers snuggled close together. Morrison was the successful proprietor of the Benton General Store. She was a native of Pennsylvania and had come to Benton to be near her brother, Henry. Henry came west to seek his fortune as a miner, but had since gone to work as a clerk in Morrison's store.

They both realized it was time to head to town following what had become a regular Sunday afternoon affair. Bob enjoyed sharing his knowledge of this high desert region with Sarah. Usually they settled back in one of the hot springs for which the area was known. But this Sunday, he took her to the Crags, a series of interesting geological rock formations not too far from Benton.

## Gun Play at Convict Lake

Nineteen year old Sarah was still a bit of a tom-boy. With 125 pounds spread over her 5'6" frame, she posed a striking figure. Her long Irish reddish brown hair, freckles and sparkling green eyes accentuated her beautiful face. Her skin was smooth and radiant. But Bob was really impressed that her beauty was not just skin deep. She had a good heart and a deep passion.

"Hey," he chuckled to himself, "she was a great cook too." Bob noted he gained a few pounds since they began hanging out together. Today they shared a wonderful picnic. As the wagon wound its way down the steep incline, they looked forward to the evening ahead. Henry Devine, Sarah's brother, was having a dinner party in their honor to announce their upcoming wedding.

In the bustling mining town of Aurora about 15 miles from Bodie, the Poor family was feeling anything but that. Today they had been enjoying a long awaited reunion with their son William. His dad was the proprietor of a local hotel in Aurora and his mom kept busy raising his brothers and sisters. Billy, as his friends called him, had been living in California. He was thrilled when he received a recent letter from his dad telling about him a job that was opening up with family friend. Billy Wilson operated both stage and mail routes in western Nevada and was looking for a rider that he could rely on to cover an important mail route.

Young Billy was an excellent horseman. He was ready to try something else. He'd move on to a new life of excitement in the "wild west." Billy was excited. He really looked forward to his first trip for Wilson on Tuesday.

Meanwhile back at the prison, the Captain of the Guard Volney Rollins, called to the prisoners to get ready to return to their cells. As Rollins turned the key in the lock, many prisoners, waited, as if spring loaded, for the signal that was to given. It did not come. Rollins started to swing the heavy iron door open. He stepped back. There was a momentary pause. Some of them thought "What now"? Never at a loss for action, Morton decided

## Gun Play at Convict Lake

to take the lead and got the game underway by yelling:

"Now, let's go now. Let's get the hell out of here!"

Suddenly all hell broke loose. John Squires forcefully opened the iron door. He seized Rollins and threw him to the sawdust covered floor. Others flowed through the open door like water escaping through a hole in a dam. Seeing Squires with Rollins, fellow prisoner William Russell pulled Rollins' head by the hair. Squires grabbed a bottle and swung it at the Captain's head. He broke the bottle over Rollin's head. Blood rushed from the three and a half inch gash left by the blow.

Rollins' misfortunes were just beginning. Almost simultaneously, he was struck just over the left eye with a slung-shot, cutting his face to the bone. Now bleeding profusely, the man, wounded badly, but not mortally, sunk to the floor. Other convicts saw Rollins covered with blood and sawdust, lying helplessly and still on the floor. As they rushed in for the kill, convict Pat Hurley dragged Rollins into a cell, locked the door and threw in the key. This move more than likely saved his life.

Hearing the commotion below, the prisoners atop the roof went through the hole they had cut. They jumped down, ending up in Assistant Warden Zimmerman's room. Clad in his sleeping garments, the man awoke to a frightful scene. Dressed in his bed clothes and completely defenseless, Zimmerman could not believe his good fortune that no one noticed him. He fled down the staircase and into the courtyard.

Still upstairs, Morton, Jones, Clifford and Thomas Ryan led others to the armory. They broke in. For their efforts they were rewarded with two Henry rifles, two boxes of rifle cartridges, four double barreled shotguns and several six-shooters. Jones and Morton each took a Henry and a box of cartridges. For good measure they also tucked a pistol in their pants. Thomas Flynn grabbed a revolver and some bullets. The shotguns and other pistols were grabbed up.

Now armed with Henry rifles, Morton and Jones were very dangerous. They went downstairs to the prison's main door. It was open. They saw someone running toward the Warm Springs Hotel. Some convicts were making a run for the sagebrush. It was

## Gun Play at Convict Lake

dusk and the blowing wind had cut the visibility noticeably. They decided to wait a few minutes before venturing out.

Knowing a third Henry rifle was missing, Ryan figured it was in the Warden's quarters. Leading a group of convicts, Ryan set out to get the weapon from Denver. He had no idea that it was out of service and in the warder's office, waiting for repairs. Ryan stopped when he saw Denver and Dedman at the top of the stairs. Clifford was right behind him. With only his Derringer to defend himself, Denver pointed it at the convicts menacingly. The surge towards him didn't stop. He fired and hit Clifford point blank. The others fell back. Clifford clutched his stomach.

Seeing Clifford go down, Ryan yelled for more men to assist them in getting the weapon from the warden. He urged them to rush the warden and Dedman. He wanted that extra Henry rifle. For some reason several fellow convicts blindly followed his orders with disastrous results. Denver had retreated to his bedroom where he grabbed a loaded revolver. Returning to the main room he saw Dedman has his hands full. The orderly had broken an oak chair into kindling and was using the largest piece to strike anyone that tried to come through the door.

Seeing that no progress was being made, Ryan was furious. He wanted control of that third Henry rifle. He was adamant in his resolve. He figured the convicts needed it to secure their freedom once they finally left the prison. He swore to those around him that Denver had it with him in his quarters.

"Throw down that Henry rifle warden," yelled Ryan up to Denver. "Quit being stupid and throw it down. When you do, we'll leave. No harm will come to you."

Denver heard this request. He knew the rifle wasn't with him. He last saw it in the office. He couldn't meet Ryan's request even if he wanted to. But he figured if he could stall the prisoners, help will soon come from outside the prison.

"No," the warden replied.

"Shoot him, shoot the warden," Ryan screamed. "Shoot him and we can walk up and get the Henry."

Denver got hit in the hip and thrown back. Though wounded and in immense pain, he somehow got up. He planted himself

## Gun Play at Convict Lake

just inside the door and stared right at Ryan, revolver in hand.

"If you want the damn rifle, why don't you just come on up and get it," chided the warden.

Ryan and the others left. In addition to his bullet wound, Denver suffered wounds caused by two slung-shot blows to the head. These scalp bleed wounds profusely. He most likely would have been killed if not for the assistance Dedman gave him. Dedman was covered with cuts, bruises and abrasions. He sat down on the floor physically drained.

In Benton Hot Springs, Henry Devine toasted the upcoming wedding of his sister Sarah to Bob Morrison. The three were among several friends gathered together for the formal announcement of the wedding plans. George Hightower, his wife Martha, along with James McLaughlin and his wife Mary, were among the prominent citizens of Benton Hot Springs in attendance.

Morrison, a native of New York, came to nearby Owensville around 1863. He partnered with some other men in a couple of early mining adventures. He had since expanded his holdings and now owned the Benton General Store. The 34 year-old was assigned the responsibility of regional Wells Fargo agent this past

year. Sarah kept house for her brother, a task she would soon be doing for Robert or Bob as most folks called him.

Her first glimpse of Bob took place several months ago soon after she arrived in Benton. She saw a fine figure of a man at a distance on the steps in front of the General Store. She met him later in the week. Henry gave her a list and asked her to run to the

## Gun Play at Convict Lake

store for him. As Sarah entered the store suddenly there he was. He was writing down an order for an older woman at the counter. The lady had chosen a selection of mail order household goods offered by FA Walker and Co. This tall, handsome man was soft spoken and appeared gentle. She liked that he appeared taller than she, about 5'11" and 160 pounds, she guessed. Bob was well put together. Sarah decided to look through some of the order books on hand while she waited her turn. She saw stoves offered by Rathbone and Kennedy as well as Potter and Co. The Singer Sewing Machine catalogue interested her too. She was looking through the Christmas presents offered in the James P. Walke book. Suddenly she realized his attention shifted to her, she nearly melted when she looked into his deep blue eyes.

Robert Morrison

"Good morning young lady. May I help you?" She barely heard him say to her. Sarah looked down and stumbled for words. She blushed a bright pink. Bob was equally taken with her.

"I need to buy a few things," she blurted.

"Well you came to the right place," he said teasing her, "we actually sell a few things."

They both laughed and exchanged introductions. Their bond grew steadily every day. She was so proud of the man that would soon be her husband. They planned to have a big family. She loved children. She already had names picked out, Robert, of course, for the first boy. She was currently looking forward to her upcoming trip to Los Angeles to visit her relatives from Pennsylvania this next week. She was excited about her planned marriage to Bob, which would take place shortly after she returned near the end of the month. There was so much to do.

Sarah Devine

# Gun Play at Convict Lake

## All Hell Breaks Loose

Guard Ed Langlois was relaxing on his day off when he heard screams coming from the prison yard. Muffled sounds of pop, pop, pop came to him as well. He stepped into his quarters where he grabbed his rifle and six shooter. He filled his pockets with cartridges. He stepped out of his quarters and ran into the yard. He was known as a brave man and his actions over the next 15 minutes would attest to that reputation. Another off duty guard, F.M. Isaacs saw Langlois in the fight. Not having his own weapon and knowing it would be very dangerous to try and get it, he ran up behind him and took Ed's rifle so he could join the fight. He backed off about 30 paces from the guard room window. Inside he saw several prisoners trying to break out. He did not recognize any of them. He saw two standing on the front porch of the prison shooting at anything that did not look like a convict. He could not tell who it was because it was nearly dark. He fought bravely this hour. His shots were very effective. Close by, Langlois, after reloading and firing several times, ran out of bullets. For some reason he grabbed a club and ran into the midst of the fleeing convicts.

Nearby, Matt Pixley and his wife were finishing their supper at the Warm Springs Hotel. Although adjacent to the Nevada State Prison, the hotel was in a very peaceful setting. So they were naturally astounded to hear a tremendous commotion in the courtyard, along with terrible, frightening screams. Pixley told his wife to lock herself in their bedroom. He'd go see what was happening. He quickly peered through the window and was amazed to see convicts scurrying about the courtyard with the Warden's daughter, Jennie, in the middle of it all. He immediately realized an escape attempt was underway. Running across his living room, he grabbed two pistols from the bureau drawer. "Damn," he thought, "why don't I keep these loaded." He emptied a box of

## Gun Play at Convict Lake

cartridges on the table and quickly loaded each one. He headed towards the front door knowing he had to rescue Jennie. He was a very brave man. His timing could not have been worse.

He exited the door and stood on the porch trying to determine his next move. Still inside the prison, Charles Jones shattered a window with his rifle barrel. In the fading light he saw a man with two pistols in his hand on the Warm Springs Hotel porch. "That just won't do," Charlie thought. He raised his weapon and sighted on Pixley. Thomas Flynn had already exited the prison and likewise saw someone on the hotel porch with pistols in hand. He also realized this threat to himself and the others. He made sure a cartridge was in the chamber and sighted in on Pixely as well. Two shots rang out. A bullet caught Pixley just below the left eye, knocking him back into the hotel wall killing him instantly. No one ever knew for sure whether Jones or Flynn fired the fatal shot. It really didn't matter; a brave young man lay dead on the hotel steps. It was reported that the grief displayed by his young wife at seeing his lifeless body was "heart rending." Jones chambered another round. Flynn reloaded. The peaceful early evening surrounding the prison had been entirely disrupted.

Off duty guards dropped what they were doing and came to join the fight. The Warm Springs Hotel bartender, Burgesser, heard the gunshots. He headed to the window to see what was going on. He was sickened by the sight of Pixley dead on the porch. He grabbed the double barrel shotgun along with a box of shells from beneath the bar and entered the fight. Matt had been his friend. He was immediately grazed in each ear by two errant shots. He fought on. A third shot tore into the crotch of his pantaloons, ripping away the whole seat of his pants as well as his drawers. Drafty, but undaunted, he continued to battle back.

Convict Ed Goyette didn't know what to do. Did he take advantage of this turmoil and slip out? Or did he lay low and stay here? In the midst of this thought he saw the Warden's daughter Jennie. The little girl was holding her hands over her face as if to shelter her from all that was happening. Bullets were flying everywhere. Fate took over. Goyette ran to the child and swept her up in his arms and carried her to a safe place. *Good man deep inside.*

## Gun Play at Convict Lake

Gunfire in the yard was brutal. Burgesser saw Isaacs go down. He knew the man would not survive in the open. He rushed over to the fallen guard to render assistance. Goyette also saw Isaacs' situation was extremely dangerous. He worked his way over to help the bartender drag the wounded man to cover.

Johnny Newhouse, another guard, heard all the noise and

was happy to join in the gun battle with no regard for his own safety. With a pistol in each hand, he was really having a great time. He took a bead on a striped figure trying to escape across the yard. Newhouse rose up to fire again and was hit both in the upper back and the back of the head. The force of the slugs knocked him off his feet. On the ground and losing consciousness, he was no longer a threat to the escapees.

Hanging around outside the prison, Joseph Parasich, another guard, could not help but hear the gun fire erupting and the screaming coming from inside. Joe ran across to the Warm Springs Hotel. He searched around for a weapon. He located a revolver and a box of cartridges. He quickly loaded it. He stuck

## Gun Play at Convict Lake

more bullets in his pockets. He ducked out the hotel and entered the yard with his gun blazing. He could see the results of his fire taking place. Suddenly he was sickened by the sound of a ball hitting him in the groin. The bullet traveled some distance in fleshy tissue and lodged between the femur bone and nearby artery. Luckily it didn't sever the artery. His wound was very bad. He writhed in agony near the prison door.

Langlois, the brave Frenchman, along with Burgesser were the only deterrents remaining. Neither had any ammunition left. Langlois had been grazed by so many balls that his clothing had been cut to shreds. Realizing their fight was futile, they entered the prison to see what assistant they could render there.

Jones, the barrel of his Henry rifle hot to the touch, rested the gun on his shoulder. Behind him, Morton and Black noticed the absence of gunfire. It was apparent to these murderous men that there was no one left to stop them from simply walking out. Many of the other prisoners had no stomach for the killing and fighting that had been taking place. They had kept safe in the cover of the prison until seeing it was prudent to leave. They now realized that there was no one left to stop them from walking right out and into the darkness.

Jones managed to remove his irons. As he shuffled along outside the prison, he casually glanced down at Pixley. He smiled for a moment. "Better him than me!" Charlie saw Newhouse and Isaacs badly wounded. He didn't like seeing these men in their present condition. Another prisoner, Pruitt, watching from across the yard, saw Jones walking over to Newhouse. He couldn't believe it when Jones pointed the muzzle of the rifle at the wounded man's head. With his finger on the hammer, he moved it back so it was ready to fire. Pruitt wanted to yell or something, he was simply in shock that a man would do such a thing. Jones was about to put Newhouse out of his misery. To Pruitt's relief, another convict grabbed the barrel and moved it away from the man's head.

"That man fought bravely. If his wounds kill him, that's one thing, but to shoot him like a dog is wrong. Besides, you might need the ammunition later today or tomorrow."

Prone on the ground Newhouse barely understands what

## Gun Play at Convict Lake

had just transpired. Fate has stepped in and neither he nor Isaacs would be assassinated tonight. Pruitt shook his head.

Nearly twenty-five men smiled wearily as they trudged away from that horrible place. Soon several men in small groups or by themselves split off from the main party. They would find their own way. The main body of men turned to the right so they would reach the Carson River. When the party reached the water, it had thinned considerably. At Clifford's suggestion the group rose up and headed south up the river. It was around 9:30 pm when they approached the cabin at what was called the Mexican Dam. It was quiet, but the escapes were very weary. Clifford and Jones huddled together for a moment. Then Clifford stood up.

"I need three men to go up and see who's at the cabin."

"I'm game," said Burke

"Me too," Flynn said.

"I'm with ya," said Squires.

"Give me a whistle when the coast is clear."

The three men went ahead to make sure it was safe for the rest of them. Seeing a light in the cabin, these scouts quietly crept toward the cabin. Suddenly a dog barked a warning. The men froze. The cabin door swung open and a tall man peered outside. The hound continued his barking.

"Quit that barkin dog," yelled the figure in the doorway.

The big hound, his tail waggin away, stopped as commanded to do so by his master. The man walked outside. The scouts saw he was unarmed.

"Anyone out here," inquired the man?

"Good evening there partner, no need to be concerned, we don't mean you any harm," Burke called to the man.

A shrill whistle brought the other men to the cabin. It was home to a blacksmith that made his living tending to the needs of the local ranchers and teamsters in the region. Six of the convicts had not yet been able to get out of their chains.

"Obviously, we're in a lot of trouble," said Clifford. "Some of these men need to get their irons off. I need you to get that done."

"I reckon I can get that done," said the big man. "Follow

## Gun Play at Convict Lake

me on down to the shop."

The blacksmith was followed to his shop by the six men still shackled. Some of the others sat and rested. A couple entered the cabin to see what they might be able to use. At the shop the big fella gathered up his chisel and a small sledge hammer. He pointed to his anvil.

"Here," he said to young Roberts, the first man in line, "put you wrist up there."

The boy nervously followed his instruction. The blacksmith turned a chain link to the position he wanted. His huge muscles bulged and a single swing of the hammer split the chain link. The boy pulled his arm free and rubbed his sore wrist. He was pleased.

"Thanks mister," said Roberts.

"No problem son. All right, who's next?"

Bedford Roberts

In less than 20, the men were free. It was around midnight when the men rose up as a unit and slowly disappeared into the night. When the main body of men left the Mexican Dam, they all traveled down stream. About a half mile below the dam, they crossed the river. They moved away from the water and up a hill in an easterly direction. After awhile one man suggested splitting into smaller parties so it would be harder for a posse to track them. It was agreed that this was a good idea.

After awhile only 10 remained. This group was composed of Clifford, Parsons, Roth, Chapman, Burke, Jones, Morton, Black, Cockerell and Roberts. No one moved.

"All right," said Jones, assuming command, "let's get out of here."

A few miles into the Pine Nut range, Morton stopped the party. He turned to Jones and loudly demanded to know when they would turn and head straight toward Bishop Creek. Jones had told him they would be able to

Charles Jones

## Gun Play at Convict Lake

get help from his friends there. Back in prison Charlie had shared letters with Lea from a Mrs. Hutchinson, who lived in Bishop Creek. Jones said that this lady and other friends he had there would help him once he got there. Jones looked around the group of men in the party. He did not like the way Morton brought up the current topic of discussion. The last thing he wanted was for these men to know anything about what he had in mind. Realizing he has to answer Morton's question, Jones purposely said he was pretty sure they were close to the turn off point. The "pretty sure" comment got the response he wanted from many of the men in the group.

Leandor Morton

"Hell", Parsons said, "Bishop Creek's a long ways off!"

"If you're not sure, I'm not going that way," added Roth.

Several others uttered an agreement.

"I don't care who comes with me," Jones sneered. "If most of you were dead or dying back there it wouldn't bother me."

Parsons and Roth looked at each other in utter amazement. Chapman mumbled something to Clifford.

"Lighten up Charlie," said Lea. "We're in this together."

"I wasn't talking about you Lea," replied Jones. "I know I can count on you. You were blazing away back there. Others were too. But I don't recall seeing any of them over there until the gun fire stopped."

Parsons and Clifford took great offense at this comment. Roth was standing apart with Roberts. Clifford turned towards Charlie and said:

"Sorry ya feel that way Charlie. I got myself shot and Parsons was wounded too. I'm not sure you know what you're talking about. But hey, no hard feelings. I wish you luck."

With that said he turned and addressed the others.

"A friend of mine has a ranch, not too far away from here. We can be there in a couple days. It's a hell of lot closer than Bishop Creek. Anyone that wants to come with me is welcome."

"I'm with you Frank," mumbled Roth.

"Me too," said Parsons.

## Gun Play at Convict Lake

"Count me in," Chapman said.

No one else said a word. With that Clifford started off into the darkness. Chapman, Parsons, Roberts and Roth turned and followed him.

The "Jones Gang" at this point included Morton, Cockerell, Black and Burke. After Roberts moved away with Clifford's bunch, Cockerell yelled after him.

"Hey, Bedford, don't go along with them. Charlie's got a great plan. Get back here!"

Roberts heard him. Tilden Cockerell was a very good friend of Roberts' dad Chat. Chat had a stage station in Long Valley near Susanville, California. He knew the boy looked forward to robbing stages. When just 17, he and Charles Beaver, who was even younger, stopped a coach. After demanding the driver throw down his shotgun, Beaver kept a shaky six shooter on the coach. Roberts dismounted to take whatever he could get from the passengers. As the heist was unfolding, the driver correctly read the characters behind the masks as completely inexperienced highway men.

Tilden Cockerell

While the outlaws were busy with their quarry, the driver slowly and carefully reached for the concealed Derringer located in his breast pocket. Fingering the tiny weapon, in one quick motion he drew, cocked and fired the weapon. The shot hit young Charles, knocking him off his mount. The gunfire spooked both horses. They ran off into the darkness. While the driver reloaded, Roberts fled the scene. His gravely wounded accomplice was left to die in the sagebrush or be captured. The horses had not run far. Roberts retrieved his mount about 50 yards from the coach. It was then he realized he had dropped the stolen loot. Stepping aboard his horse, he gathered up the reigns of his companion's mount and went home. Beaver survived and turned in Roberts.

He mulled over what Tilden had been saying. 'Why not tie in with guys that seemed to have a plan." He turned around and walked with his mentor back to join the Jones' gang.

# Gun Play at Convict Lake

## A Trek Through the Pine Nut Mountains

Jones kept moving along as silently as he could. Cockerell had a tough time trudging along without shoes. Charles thought to himself "it was good to have people fear you." He knew the others were aware of his actions during the break. He heard whispers about his near execution of the guard on the ground in the yard. He knew the men in his party were also leery of Morton. That worked well to his advantage too. The two of them should be able to lead these other mutts safely out of the Pine Nut Range. He figured they would travel through the Adobe Valley and skirt around Aurora. They would closely follow the Aurora Owens River Toll Road to Long Valley in Mono County. From there it was just a few more miles to Bishop Creek where he figured help would be available to him. Then they would slip up and over the Sierra.

Abruptly Charlie stopped. The wind had shifted. His nose detected the scent of a campfire. He sniffed the early morning breeze turning his head to help pinpoint the direction of the fire. He figured the source was about a quarter mile ahead. His companions had smelled the smoke as well. Charlie and Morton lead the way as the party of men altered their course and headed into the wind. Soon they observed a low glow ahead of them. As they moved forward they could see the faint outline of a freight wagon silhouetted by the fire. A team of horses was tethered to the wagon. They watched a moment to see if they could tell how many men might be at the camp. No movement was observed. They couldn't tell if anyone was asleep on the ground.

Suddenly, embers flickered into the air. They heard a sound. They could see someone that was partly hidden by the wagon was stoking the fire. One of the horses sensed their presence and whinnied. Another pawed the ground. The man stood up and looked around. Charlie's group saw the outline of a rifle resting against the wagon wheel. The man told the horses to settle

## Gun Play at Convict Lake

down. Charlie whispered that he and Morton were going to rush the man. He ordered them to stay put. Morton and Jones inched forward. Just feet from the wagon they rushed him. He was tackled by Morton as he dove for the weapon. The teamster, a Dutchman, struggled with his assailant, loudly cussing him in broken English. The others came in to help. Burke and Roberts dragged the old man over to the wagon. Morton dusted himself off. Black grabbed a rope from the wagon and secured him to the wheel.

"Hell, why did ya tie him up," Morton said. "He shouldn't be tied up. Kill him. Once I tied up this bastard, real tight too. What'd I get for being merciful? I ended up with 19 buckshot pellets in my back for not killing a man that I had left tied up."

"We don't need to kill him," said Burke. "That's the best way to get more people riled up about us. Now we just have the law after us. We don't need citizens after us too. Think about it."

Cockerell and the others were cold. He told Roberts to build up the fire. Black had gone through the wagon to see what they could use He found an old rifle, two six shooters and some clothes. The men tried on the clothes to see who could wear the stuff they found. They knew it was important to quickly get out of the prison duds. All the while Jones was looking over the stock. They looked good. Charlie came over to the camp.

"Well boys," he laughed, "we got ourselves some horses.

&§&§&§

Billy Poor was very happy. He spent the night in a very comfortable feather bed. Today his dad would show him the town. Aurora was a bustling place. He looked forward to their day together. He was also very excited about his new job. There was no danger from Indians. No one was going to try and rob a mail rider. His day dream was ended by his mother's request he join them for breakfast. He sat down to a huge plate of pancakes with three over easy eggs nestled on top. She remembered he thought. As he did when he was a kid, Billy poked the yokes with his fork. He liked the yoke to spill all over his pancakes. Most folks preferred syrup. If any pancakes remained after the yokes disappeared, he would just add syrup to the pile.

## Gun Play at Convict Lake

❦❦❦

Robert Morrison was not looking forward to this day. Sarah had made plans to visit some relatives in Los Angeles. Today she would leave. He would take her to the stage that travels from Aurora to Fish Slough around noon at Adobe Meadows.

"Good morning," she said.

"Hi honey," he replied, as he kissed her full on the lips.

The energy created by the meeting of their flesh swept through them both. It was good they were to be married shortly. One or both may burst if this union were to be postponed much longer. He helped her into the wagon. She adjusted herself as he climbed in himself. He unwrapped the reins and urged the horse onward. The next few days would be hard on them both. Not knowing what to say, neither said anything. He looked to the north when they heard the rumbling sounds of the stage coming over the rise. The coach slowed to a stop followed by a cloud of dust. They had both turned there heads to avoid a mouthful.

"Howdy, Pete."

"Hi there, Bob."

Sarah remained seated as Bob took the luggage. She looked up at Pete and smiled.

"Good morning. You'll have to forgive Bob. He's so preoccupied with me leaving that he's lost his manners. I'm Sarah."

"Pleased to make your acquaintance young lady."

Bob helped lift Sarah from the wagon. He gently set her on the ground. They looked deeply into each other's eyes. Both were a bit moist with sadness. They shared a big hug and several goodbye kisses. Then, he assisted her as she climbed aboard.

"See ya soon Sarah. Make sure you keep that thing on the road, Pete. You have someone very valuable to me aboard."

"Sure enough Bob."

The big coach started on down the wide road. Bob's heart felt heavy as he climbed back into the wagon by himself. He watched for a moment as the stage rolled up the road. Sarah looked over her head and waved at Bob. He saw her turn and wave. Raising his hand, he waved back. He was a bit embarrassed. He was

## Gun Play at Convict Lake

too old to have tears in his eyes. Morrison arrived back at Benton and left his wagon at the livery stable. He dusted himself off and headed over to the General Store. Henry saw Bob come in.

"Howdy Bob, you get sis off on time?"

"Yeah."

"While you were out a package from San Francisco arrived for you. It's over there under the cash register."

Bob hung up his coat. He went over to retrieve the package. He expected that it was his new suit. "Well Henry, it looks pretty good. What do you think?" Said Bob, holding up the coat.

"It looks awfully formal. I think Sarah will be pleased with you all dressed up in that outfit."

"She better, it sure did cost enough."

"Oh well, you only get married once."

"I guess so. I'll probably get buried in it too!"

∂∂∂

Nearly 100 miles to the south, Sarah pulled the covers around her as she settled in for a good night sleep. She longed for Bob's comforting hug. Soon she would not have to sleep by herself anymore. She knew she was ready for him. Their future was secure. Look at what Bob had already accomplished. She fell asleep thinking of his gentle arms around her.

∂∂∂

The posse following the Jones Gang was hot on their trail. It was fast going for their Indian guide to follow them through the sand hills. But when they got to the rocky ridges, he had to proceed much more slowly. In the mountains they found the Dutchman. In his broken English he told them he figured his assailants were probably five or six hours ahead of them. It was late in the day when the posse left, the Dutchman went with them.

The Indian tracked the convicts until some time after dark. It was obvious to the group that no one could track them over this long rocky ridge. The experienced guide looked at the stars above him. He scanned the distant mountain peaks. In broken English he said he had a hunch where the men went. Three or four miles

## Gun Play at Convict Lake

ahead of them, well up the side of a rugged peak, was a spring. He figured the convicts would go there.

The men wanted to stop and rest. The leaders insisted they move on. So the group followed the Indian through the dark. He led them over rocks and through sagebrush. They went over precipices at the risk of life or limb. At length, after much misgiving amongst posse members, the Indian stopped at the spring. Atchison told the party they would rest here until daybreak.

After stopping at a spring for about an hour, Jones took his party through Pine Valley. The six neared Hot Springs on the Walker River in the early morning. Charlie knew he was about 10 miles north of Wellington on the Dayton Road. The horses they took from the Dutchman helped them make better progress. They were in good spirits. Charlie started toward the outpost.

"Rest here, boys. I'll go in and get us a few things."

He had some coins they had stolen from the Dutchman so he could carry on a regular transaction. This would lessen any suspicion of them. Charlie hoped to put off anyone on his track while he was here. He saw the proprietor behind the counter.

"Excuse me sir, how far is it to Dayton?"

The man gave him the directions he needed. Charlie thanked the elderly gentleman and walked out the door. "Man, I sure can be personable when I need to," Charlie thought to himself. Jones then led his band down the road toward Dayton.

"This isn't the way to Bishop Creek," said Cockerell.

## Gun Play at Convict Lake

"We're heading north. Bishop Creek is south."

"Shut up, Tilden," commanded Charlie. "I'm trying to get anyone interested in us to follow this track from Hot Springs towards Dayton. So just shut your mouth and try to keep up."

They left plain tracks to Dayton for a couple miles. He felt anyone following will take the bait and track them to Dayton. At this point the party turned about. They would now pass north and then east. This would take him near Pine Grove and then on the Aurora Road between Wellington and Sweetwater.

⊰⊱⊰⊱⊰⊱

Ben Lackey arose from a deep sleep at first light. For a moment he just lay there on his bedroll, trying to gather his senses. He did not recall where he was. He had not ever seen the place during daylight. He pulled his boots on and stood up to answer nature's call. He walked a few yards from the camp. Watching the morning sky as he took care of business, he was shocked when he looked down. There, not 10 feet from where he slept, were signs of the convicts' tracks.

"Hey," he yelled. "Wake up. Look what I found."

Their guide quickly verified what Lackey had seen. He said the tracks were about six hours old. The posse saddled up and set off after the Indian. He was already a quarter mile ahead.

⊰⊱⊰⊱⊰⊱

Billy Poor awoke to the noise of an early morning rooster. He rose from his comfortable feather bed. Barefoot, he wandered outside to make use of the little shed with the half moon on the door. Back inside his mother had hot coffee on the stove. He poured himself a cup.

"Morning ma. That is a mighty loud old bird out there."

"That he is, son. I've got breakfast for ya. Your father had to leave late last night. His night clerk got sick so he had to cover for him. He said he'd see you tonight after you get back."

The young man was very excited. Today he would take his first trip as a mail rider for Billy Wilson. He knew he did not have to be there till noon. However, he was going early for no other

## Gun Play at Convict Lake

reason than he was really excited! His mother had another pile of pancakes covered with three fried eggs, just as he liked them.

Billy got dressed and pulled on his boots. He took the new gloves his father gave him out of the box. He stuck them in his saddle bag. They were great. They even had his initials on them! He was going to take the morning stage from Aurora to the Sweetwater station to meet Wilson. He kissed his mother good bye. He walked up the street to the stage office.

In Independence, Sarah was up early, ready to head to Los Angeles. She had not seen her relatives for over a year. She was anxious to get started. The stage from Independence was scheduled to leave at 9. Just think, by tomorrow I will be having dinner with my family. I have so much to tell them about Bob. She then realized she had not thought about him at all for the past two hours. That was the first time that happened since she met him!

⁂

Those trailing Jones and his five comrades reached the Hot Springs on the Walker River in the early morning. The weary men dismounted. They looked forward to a hot meal and black coffee. They were served beans, eggs and tortillas. They asked a young Mexican boy to water the horses. If possible, they wanted them fed too. While eating, the officers learned the six convicts had passed that point sometime after midnight. They found they were still six hours behind their quarry. It was reported they had set out for Dayton to the east. Sheriff Swift told his group to mount up, they were turning back. Wishing the others good luck, Swift and his men were on their way.

Ben Lackey was driven. He was a bulldog. He wanted to catch these men. Atchison was not sure. Downey and the Virginia militia leader sided with Lackey. The Dutchman was hell bent to stay on the convicts' trail. The men had been able to give the horses water and feed, plus a little more than an hour's rest. They thanked the Hot Springs proprietor for his hospitality and hit the trail. They headed east toward Dayton. Jones was smart, but not smart enough to fool experienced trackers. They saw where Charlie had turned south. They followed.

## The Unfortunate Billy Poor

The stage arrived at Sweetwater at 10. Young Billy quickly stepped off the coach. The driver threw down Billy's saddlebags. He had told him where to meet with Mr. Wilson. Billy could feel his heart pounding as he opened the door to the man's office and entered. The man behind the desk sized the young fellow up.

"Why I imagine you're young Poor. Welcome to Sweetwater. You're a mite early, son. Come on in. Sit down."

"Thanks. I just wanted to get off on the right foot. I'm really excited about this opportunity."

"Well we have plenty of time to go over everything."

Billy looked around the man's office. Aside from a desk and the wood stove, he saw wall maps and posted announcements. He noticed one of them told about a Nevada State Prison break at Carson City this past Sunday night.

Wilson took Poor to the stable. He asked him to pick a mount. He did. Poor asked Wilson which saddle and tack belonged to the horse. Wilson liked the kid. He knew enough that the horse would be paired with a saddle. Poor led the horse over to the office and tied it to the rail. Wilson gave him the mail pouch. Poor tied it to this saddle. He checked his cinch and tightened it. He patted the animal that was about to speed him on his way.

Billy opened his saddle bag and took out the gloves his dad had given him. He pulled them on. He grabbed the saddle horn, swung onto the horse and rode out.

≈≈≈

The Jones gang had passed Pine Grove, skirted Wellington and was now on the Aurora Road moving toward Sweetwater.

"Hey Morton," said Charlie, "doesn't that guy Dingman ride the mail on this trail?"

"Yeah, I think he does, last time I heard anyway."

## Gun Play at Convict Lake

"Wouldn't it be great if he happened along today?"

"That would definitely make my day."

He was hated by the inmates. During a failed 1870 breakout, three convicts were killed. It was said Dingman killed them. But two were killed by Wellington Bower. Dingman did get one.

No matter - in typical prison bravado, they had vowed to kill the man if ever had the chance.

❧❧❧

Ben Lackey's horse came up lame. He stopped and checked his mount. The news was not all bad. The horse had thrown a shoe and picked up a rock. Ben removed the rock. He knew he could not continue trying to catch men so far ahead with this horse.

"Damn, the luck. I can't go any further on this horse."

Downey, Atchison and the Virginia militia leader looked around their combined group. It was evident that none of them should go on.

"Well, Ben," said Downey, "this must be some sort of sign. We had all better head back."

With that Downey, Atchison, Lackey and the rest slowly rode east toward Dayton. It was closer than Carson City.

❧❧❧

The Jones gang had stopped to rest, again. These frequent stops were caused by Cockerell. Charlie knew Cockerell's feet were in terrible shape. He could see the man was barely able to walk. This was slowing down their movement considerably. He needed time to think. He took Burke aside.

"You know that we'd be better off if Tilden just stayed here by himself," said Charlie.

"What do you mean?" Inquired Burke.

"He can hardly walk and is slowing us up. We need to get rid of him. I think I'll just shoot him. That'll solve the problem."

Burke was shocked. He walked over to Cockerell to try and prevent Jones from taking any action. Jones dropped the subject.

"We're gonna rest here awhile," said Charlie. "Roberts take a horse and scour around to see if you can find anything to

## Gun Play at Convict Lake

eat or anything of use to us. But don't be gone too long."

"All right Charlie. I won't be long."

Bedford rode toward Sweetwater. About a mile from the others, he saw a small structure about 50 yards from the road. He cautiously rode up.

"Hello the house." No one answered. He dismounted and tied his horse to a post. "Anyone here." Again no answer. He opened the front door and entered the house. Roberts looked around the place. In the bedroom was an old cedar chest. Inside were several articles of clothing. The kid quickly stripped off his prison duds and put on a pair of pants and a shirt. He gathered up the rest of the clothes for the others. He left the house and headed for the barn. He figured he had been there about five minutes. He heard something out on the road. It was hoof beats. Someone was coming from the south. He hid himself in the cornfield. He watched as a single rider approached and rode on past.

Billy Poor was enjoying his ride. It was a pretty day and not too hot. His mount was an easy ride. The gait was comfortable. Billy was not getting sore. He had been a little worried about that. He had not ridden much for the past couple of years. He had saddle sores before and they were no fun. Billy was now about twelve miles out from Sweetwater. The actual spot was a half mile north of Sulfur Springs.. He saw a stream crossing the road. He

## Gun Play at Convict Lake

slowed to a walk. Perhaps he would water the horse. He looked up and saw a group of men.

Burke was the first to hear the rider.

"Hey, maybe that's Dingham!"

The rider slowed down and was riding toward them.

"Afternoon," Billy said politely.

Morton reached up and pulled Billy off the horse. The kid landed hard on the ground. Morton held him there with a knee on his chest. He took a six shooter from the Billy's belt, tossing it to Jones. Billy looked up at the others watching him. He was petrified. Morton went through his pockets. He found $20 in coins and a pen knife. Seeing two rings on the man's fingers, Morton removed them. He then stood and pulled Billy up. The frightened boy was wild eyed.

Burke sized him up. "What's your name? You look like that bastard on the jury that helped convict me."

"Poor," gasped Billy, "Billy Poor. I'm a mail rider."

"That's it. You look just like your old man. That bastard was on the jury that sent me to prison. I'd like to murder you son, just to make your old man suffer for what he did to me!"

"Where's the regular mail rider, Dingman?" Questioned Jones. "We want Dingman. We want him bad. We're gonna cook his goose!"

"There you go, you son of a bitch," Morton yelled at Jones, "you let the cat out of the bag."

"I don't know anyone named Dingman," cried Billy.

"No matter," laughed Jones. "Hey Lea, bring that guy with you and follow me."

With that, Jones walked off parallel to the road. Morton followed, dragging Poor behind him. Burke, Black and Cockerell looked on apprehensively. They figured that with the mood Charlie was in, it was better to leave him alone. They heard poor Billy, arguing for his very life, as Morton pulled him down the road. Jones stopped about 200 yards away.

"Take your boots off," ordered Morton.

"What."

"You heard me. I said take your boots off. Take your pants

## Gun Play at Convict Lake

and shirt off too."

"Why?"

"You ain't gonna need them, that's why. Hurry up."

Billy sat in the dirt tugging on his boots to pull them off. He removed his jacket, then his shirt. He stood up and undid the buttons on his pants. He slid them off. He just stood there in his long Johns. Charlie and Billy were about the same size. Jones had removed his prison shirt and pants. He took Billy clothes and put them on. He threw his prison garments at the kid.

"Here," ordered Jones "put these on."

"Why?"

"I don't want ya to catch cold!"

Billy pulled on the pants and pulled the shirt over his head. He stood there looking at Morton and Jones not knowing what to do next. Morton looked at Billy and teased him.

"Hey, aren't you one of those Nevada State Prison escapees? Maybe I better shoot you and get a reward."

For several minutes the two men took turns tormenting their captive. Billy was treated like a toy they were playing with. Finally, they tired of this sport. Jones picked up his rifle and opened the breech to see if a cartridge was ready to fire. Morton checked the rounds in his shooter. Billy's eyes showed terror as he watched his captors. Both men fired fatal shots to his head. Poor fell like a stone into the sagebrush.

"Well Lea," said Jones, "it looks like one of those convicts got what was coming to them."

"Sort of. But he doesn't look like any of us."

With that, he walked around until he found a large rock. He was barely able to lift it off the ground. Lea carried it over to the dead man and dropped it on his head.

The huge rock bounced off the dead man's head. It torn the skin on his face and broke the nose. Morton's intent was to deform the face beyond any possible recognition. This horrible act did not achieve the desired effect.

"Hell, that didn't help," said Jones, "he still looks just like the guy we killed."

"This will help," replied Morton.

## Gun Play at Convict Lake

He grabbed the dead man's legs and drug the body over next to some sagebrush. He broke off other pieces of sagebrush and put them all around the dead man's face. He pulled a match from his pocket and lit the brush on fire. In a moment it flamed up and burned rapidly.

"That'll do it," said Morton.

"Man, Lea, I never want you to get mad at me!"

Lea looked at the rings again as Jones waited to see what Lea might do next. Lea took a gold ring and tossed it to Jones..

"There you go. I'm keeping this one If I get caught, I'll just toss it away."

"Thanks. Not me. I'll wear this one to hell!"

They watched the fire play out. Morton had Poor's gloves and his boots. Then the two calmly walked back to their camp.

∼∼∼

The monthly shipment from San Francisco arrived at the Benton General Store around 11 am. Morrison and Devine had worked all morning to rearrange things. Bob wanted to make sure he had enough room for all the items he was expecting. He was glad he had lots to do.

It was hard for him not to think about Sarah. It was even harder to have to wait for a week for her return. He had grown so used to her hugs and kisses. He really missed his future wife.

"You've got that look again, Bob."

"What look is that?"

"The silly one you always get when you think about sis. She'll be back before you know it."

"Have I ever told you how pleased I am that you came out here to make your fortune? Just think, if you hadn't, Sarah would have never showed up here in Benton. Thanks, my friend."

"Ah shucks. I didn't know ya cared!"

∼∼∼

After the rider disappeared, Roberts continued to rummage around. He was able to find a few potatoes and other useful stuff. It had taken him about twenty minutes. He saw some

## Gun Play at Convict Lake

chickens and chased after them. They outmaneuvered him so he left them alone. He went back to his horse, undid the reins and climbed aboard. He took his time riding back to the others.

Upon returning to camp, he saw three men near the horses. Two others were approaching the camp from a hill nearby. He reined in to look further. He did not recognize the two coming off the hill. But soon he could tell this was Morton and Jones. Jones was no longer dressed in prison garb. Roberts asked where he got the clothes.

"Oh I got a raise. Looks like you found some duds too."

When Morton and Jones settled into camp, they told the others they had killed the mail rider.

"There the man was, begging for his life, but we didn't give him much time to beg, hey Morton?"

Burke remarked, "I don't give a cent on such cold blooded murders as that. We will have the whole country after us. I am going to leave this crowd."

"Leave if you want too," said Lea.

"I'm taking a Henry and a horse."

"You aren't taking either!"

"I'm taking both and if any of you bother me I'll shoot your guts out."

"Boys, there's no use for this," Cockerell interjected. "We've got to stick together."

John Burke

Burke sneered at the cutthroats, "You couldn't kill him with one shot, you had to shoot him twice!"

"We both shot him," said Morton, "because I had offered to pull the trigger with any man and Charlie said I'm your man. So we both shot him!"

"Hey, Burke, take these," said Morton as he threw the mail rider's boots to the man.

Then he put the mail rider's gloves on. These are brand new he thought. Nice buckskin. Burke sat down and took off his boots. He put the new ones on. Cockerell watched with interest. He had been without shoes since the break. His feet were torn up. Burke saw the man standing there.

## Gun Play at Convict Lake

"Here ya go," he said handing the old boots to Cockerell.

"It's probably best we get on down the road," said Charlie. "Hey kid, what did you find?"

"Aside from some clothes, I got a few potatoes and a couple cans of peaches."

The men had gone a short distance down the road when Morton felt his saddle move. He was aboard the mail rider's horse. He stopped and stepped down. He slipped off the mail rider's gloves so he could fix his saddle. He set them on the horse's haunch. He found the problem and worked to fix it. Satisfied his saddle was now okay, he stepped back in the stirrup and swung aboard.

A couple of hours later, perhaps 10 miles down the trail, Morton cussed out loud.

"Shit, I set those damned gloves on the back of this horse when I adjusted the saddle. They musta fallen off. I'm goin back to get them."

"That's crazy, Lea," Jones said. "Forget them."

❧❧❧

The stage agent at Wellington was mildly agitated. He had some mail that needed to go to Aurora in the morning. Normally the mail rider from Sweetheart would have been here by now. He was aware a new rider had been hired and was scheduled to work today. Where the hell was he? Some regular customers had come in to see what mail might have been delivered. He simply had to tell them the mail rider had not arrived yet. If it had been raining or snowing he could understand why the rider might be late. But today had been sunny and bright. Finally in the late afternoon, the agent walked over to the telegraph office.

"Hey there Horace," he said, "I need you to send Billy Wilson a message."

"Just a second," the man replied, fumbling with his instrument. "Okay, what's the message?"

"The mail rider from Sweetwater did not arrive yet. I have return mail to give him once he does arrive. Don't expect him until late tonight as it is now nearly 6:30."

## Gun Play at Convict Lake

Horace keyed the instrument and sent the message. The words quickly ran through the wires to Sweetwater. The telegraph operator wrote down the message and took it over to the stage office. He found the door locked and a note saying Billy had gone to Aurora for the night. Knowing Billy would want this information, the operator returned to his office and sent the information on to Aurora. The message was soon received. The Aurora clerk had seen Billy just a while ago going into the saloon just down the street. He walked over and delivered the message to Billy.

"Thanks," said Billy to the operator.

The information disturbed him. What in the hell could have happened to that boy. It was too late to go looking for him now. Well I had better go over to the Poor's place. His parents must be wondering where he was.

"Good evening Mrs. Poor. I dropped by to let you know that your son didn't get to Wellington yet. He probably had some trouble with his horse. If he doesn't turn up tonight we'll go look for him tomorrow."

"Thank you Billy, please keep me posted."

"I will. I'm sure he's just fine."

Billy walked off the porch and back toward the saloon. Mrs. Poor grabbed her shawl. She left the house and headed to the hotel. She had to tell her husband this distressing news.

⋘⋘⋘

The stage to Los Angeles had traveled a long way today. Sarah was enjoying her conversation with her fellow passengers. One was a Mr. Hopkins. He had an interesting story. Just six months ago he was nearly penniless. Then one day he was working his sluice box at some old tailings by an old abandoned mine near Monoville. To his astonishment he found 17 fairly good sized nuggets in just five hours. He packed his mule and rode to Bishop Creek. There he bought a new suit of clothes and a ticket to Los Angeles. He wanted to show his dad that he had amounted to something.

Sarah told her story too. Naturally it was mostly about Bob and what they had planned for the future. For awhile as she

## Gun Play at Convict Lake

talked about the two of them she felt very close to him.

The two other passengers were Henry Barther and Benjamin Remany, both Privates of the U.S. Cavalry. They were posted at Camp Independence. They were traveling to Los Angeles to be with Henry's mother. He had received word that his father had passed away. The elder Barthers had raised both boys back in Pennsylvania. Sarah was sad to hear of their loss, but she was pleased to hear they were fellow natives of Pennsylvania.

Having these good people to talk with during the long trip made it much more bearable. She didn't mind any of it. She just wanted to get there and see her family.

⋞⋟⋞⋟⋞⋟

"It's getting dark," said Jones as he slowed up in Dexter Canyon. "We'll stay here tonight."

Charlie dismounted. The others followed, except Cockerell, who was still afoot. The horses were hobbled. Black and Roberts looked around for some firewood. The men were hungry.

"See those cattle out there? I say we have one for dinner," said Lea pointing to the herd.

He mounted his horse and rode toward them. Soon a single shot rang out. Morton was back in about 20 minutes with some nice looking steaks.

"He Roberts, where are those potatoes you found?"

"Right here."

"Good, I'll cook them up with these steaks."

⋞⋟⋞⋟⋞⋟

Billy Poor's father took the news of his missing son hard. It was no secret to anyone in Aurora that twenty-nine convicts had escaped from the Nevada State Prison on Sunday night. Rumors had convicts going everywhere, including toward Aurora. His dad feared his son had become a victim of foul play. He shared these concerns with the sheriff and others in Aurora. Consequently a posse was gathered. It included Billy's brother Horace. The men started in pursuit around 9 that night. They rode south toward Mono Lake and Adobe Meadows.

Gun Play at Convict Lake

# Searching for the Jones' Gang

Burke was the first of the Jones Gang to awaken that morning. They had thoroughly enjoyed the beef Morton cooked last night. Cockerell woke up and wiped the sleep from his eyes. His feet were feeling better. Ever since Burke had told him what Jones had said about him dragging behind, he had been very careful. He had a shooter in his pants and would not hesitate to use it if Jones made any move to eliminate him. Roberts rolled over, farting loudly in the process. The noise actually woke Black up.

"Geeze kid, take it easy, you're gonna soil yourself," teased Burke.

"Golly boy, what crawled up your backside and died," ventured Cockerell.

Morton had been taking all this in when the wind shifted and his nose picked up what Roberts had put in the air.

"My Gawd," he said sitting up and looking at Roberts. "Get up and move away from camp if you have to do that."

Black too had a keen sense of smell. The foul odor from Robert's direction drove him from his bedroll.

"Damn, what is that?"

The object of ridicule didn't say a word. But unfortunately for the others, he was not done yet. He thought this was funny. Raising his fanny at bit, he purposely forced out another.

"Okay, Roberts," yelled Charlie, "that's enough."

"Sorry," lied Roberts. "It must be something I ate.

∽∽∽

"Fifteen miles southeast of Carson City, two prospectors, John Ludwig and John Wheeler, toiled in the hills. Like nearly everyone else, they heard of the prison break. Wheeler convinced his partner he knew how to get some of the reward money. These men were very familiar with every foot of the region.

## Gun Play at Convict Lake

"We'll cut off their escape route to Arizona and Mexico and force them back this way," said Wheeler. "I'm going to ride south to Armagosa. Once I tell the men and the Indians to be on the lookout, they'll spread the word clear to the Cajon Pass."

"That's a great idea, John. When the convicts know they can't safely go south, they head back this way. With any luck we should be able to catch a few."

They packed provisions for his ride. He mounted up. He had three swift horses. His route was nearly 150 miles one way. Wheeler spurred his mount towards Armagosa. Ludwig waved as his partner disappeared in a cloud of dust. He would gather up their gear and take it back to town. He told Wheeler he would let Sheriff Helm know of their plan. He would ride out toward the White Mountains to meet up with John on his return trip. He figured that John should be back in about a week.

∽∽∽

Down along the East Walker River, Joe Schreck looked over the beautiful land surrounding his way station 17 miles north of Aurora. He remembered the day, several years ago, when he first saw this place. There was fine bunch grass. The river provided plenty of water. "That river," he laughed to himself. "I ended up with the nickname 'Elbow Joe' just because I reside on a big bend of that old river." First, he established a stage station and then bought some cows to build up a dairy herd. "Well enough daydreaming!" He had better get the milk and butter ready for the daily stage. The stage took his products into Aurora for sale. As he finished his job, he heard his wife Julie calling him to supper.

"Elbow Joe," he thought, "you're a very lucky man!"

On the way to the station, Joe heard hoof beats. He looked up the road and saw a cloud of dust. It was too early for the stage. In a moment, he saw six men passing nearby. Five were riding, one was walking behind them. It was unusual for folks to pass by. They must be in a real hurry. He scratched his head and recalled what a rider said yesterday. Twenty nine convicts had broken out of the Nevada State Prison. Maybe these were wanted men. If so, he was glad they passed him by. He entered the house.

## Gun Play at Convict Lake

"Hi, sweetheart," he said, smiling at Julie.

"Sit down Joe. Who's out on the road?"

He didn't want to alarm her. "Who knows? But if they knew what was on this supper table they'd double back."

"Charlie," said Morton, "why are we passing this place without stopping?"

"This is Elbow Station. Joe, the owner, knows me very well. He's a great guy and has been good to me in the past."

"We should stop then," remarked Burke. "Let's have a drink and see if he has an extra horse."

"We can't stop here. It's a busy station. Someone may drop in while we're there. I'm not taking any chances. So forget it. I don't want to talk about this anymore. We just keep moving."

"Sometimes I don't know what to make of you Charlie," said Morton shaking his head. "One minute you're ready to kill everybody in sight and the next you just want to ride on by."

⊱⊱⊱

Aurora Deputy Sheriff Palmer and his posse took a detour toward Mono Lake. Eventually they were rewarded with tracks left by the convicts near Adobe Meadows. Hope that Poor was still alive rose when they found his gloves. They figured he had left them so someone following could locate him. Thus their desire to continue and help save him drove them on.

⊱⊱⊱

Billy Wilson had a restless night. He hoped the boy had not met any of the escapees on the road. There had been reports that six of the men were heading toward Aurora. If the kid did run into the convicts they probably took his horse and guns, maybe even his clothes. But what good would it do to hurt him? At first light he rode to Sweetwater. He went to the telegraph office to check for messages from Wellington. There was one.

"It's midnight. No sign of the mail rider. I'll send the mail pouch with the stage in the morning. I hope he didn't get tangled up with the six escapees heading toward Aurora."

He replied with the following:

## Gun Play at Convict Lake

"I'll find a rider to bring the mail today. If the kid doesn't show up by noon, wire me. Jim and I will set out to find him."

He asked for another message for Mr. Poor in Aurora:

"No news on Billy this morning. He's probably walking in to Wellington as you read this message. I'll send word when I know more."

Billy Wilson could not stand waiting for news about the his mail rider any longer. He found his friend Jim Peel. "Jim, I want you to come with me this afternoon. I want to ride to Wellington and see if we can find any sign of the missing mail rider. I'm worried about him."

"No problem, Billy. I'll just be a few minutes."

"Thanks Jim."

The two left the stage office in Sweetwater around noon. The men rode slowly. Each took a different side of the trail to make sure they did not miss any sign of the boy.

George Hightower stopped into the Benton General Store to pick up a freight delivery. Henry was behind the counter and Bob was helping a lady with a catalogue selection.

"Afternoon George," called out Henry. "We've got your order stacked and ready for your wagon. I'll meet around back and we'll get ya loaded. How's Martha and the kids?"

"They're fine. How's Bob with Sarah out of town?"

"Well sir, he's just plain miserable. I'll be glad when she's back and he can carry his share of the load here. Heck, I've been her longer than he has. She never bothered me like that."

"Gee, wonder why?" Laughed Hightower.

The men went around back and loaded the freight into the back of the blacksmith's wagon.

"Thanks, Henry."

"No problem George, I'll see ya later."

Morton had been riding the Billy Poor's horse since they left the scene of the boy's murder. He and the Jones gang were

## Gun Play at Convict Lake

traveling through the Adobe Meadows region. Lea quickened his pace until he was next to Charlie. "Hold up a minute."

Jones reined in his horse. "What's up, Lea?"

"I've got a bad feeling about this horse. Someone's bound to have missed that guy by now. I need to get rid of this horse. It's bound to be recognized before long."

Morton dismounted. He walked the horse over behind some outcroppings. He drew his shooter and put the barrel to the horse's head just between its' eyes. He fired. The animal fell in a hcap. It kicked and writhed for a minute and then lay still.

"Roberts, get off the horse. You can walk with Tilden."

The boy immediately dismounted. He was afraid of Lea and Charlie. There was no telling what either of them might do. They continued on till they arrived at a canyon a mile from Hightower's sawmill. Charlie led his men to the far end of the canyon. It was very secluded. There was running water and shade trees.

"I know this place," said Jones. "We'll bed down here tonight. You rest. There's a sawmill about a mile from here. I'm going up there and see about getting us something to eat. Don't go wandering off. Just stay put. I'll be back in about an hour."

Charlie turned his mount and rode off down the trail. While he was gone, more than one in this little band silently thought about heading away in a different direction. Burke, Roberts and Cockerell was very leery of Jones. Morton was just like him. The others really could not get a good read on Black. He was very quiet and kept to himself.

Charlie rode up to Hightower's sawmill late in the afternoon. He tied up his mount and looked around. He knew lots of folks here about, but didn't see any of them now. He walked over to the mess hall to see what might be available. He exchanged pleasantries with the cook. No one else was about. He asked for and obtained some bread, meat and salt. He thanked the man. Charlie mounted up and was back at his camp just before dark.

"No potatoes tonight, boys, but I did get some bread, salt and fresh meat. Hey, Lea, will you cook this up for us?"

"Glad to, Charlie. We'll eat in about an hour."

## Gun Play at Convict Lake

❧❧❧

Jim Peel and Billy Wilson arrived at Wellington three hours after they started. They had not seen any trace of Poor. They tied their horses at the hitching post in front of the stage office. Inside they found no one else had any news on the boy either.

"Well Jim, I'm going to have a drink over at the saloon. They have some good sandwich fixings there too. Then I'm going to ride to Aurora with my eye on the trail again."

"I'm with ya Billy. But it will be good to wet my whistle and get a bite to eat."

It was a frustrating ride back for Jim and Billy. They had moved along slowly criss-crossing the trail to make sure they didn't miss anything in the brush. Upon arriving in Aurora, Billy stopped at the hotel to tell Mr. Poor that he had not been to find any trace of his son. It was their he heard Sheriff Palmer had taken some men to look for the convicts and young Poor.

John Wheeler had made good time. Every time he met someone along the trail he told them to be on the lookout for the escaped convicts. He said that if they could not catch them, to try and force them to retreat back toward the Sierra or the White Mountains. He explained this concerted effort would prevent the men from fleeing to Arizona and Mexico.

He had not stopped except to water his horses and exchange mounts. He ate jerky while he rode steadily along. He

## Gun Play at Convict Lake

figured he would reach the mines by late that afternoon.

Ludwig had kept his part of the plan moving forward. He had gathered all their supplies and returned to town. He found the sheriff and laid out their plan. The sheriff was more than happy to throw in with them. He would get several more men together and figured they would need to head out about noon on Friday.

∽∽∽

Sheriff Palmer's group had terrible luck. Several posse members were sick. Perhaps it was the food they ate. Maybe they just had the ague. They were feeling awful.

"Men, we need to stop here and rest. We're after some dangerous men. Even at our best we may be no match for them."

"We can't stop now. They have my brother," said Horace Poor. "I can't stop here. I just can't. Anyone with me?"

Horace looked amongst the posse members. The sheriff looked on as well. No one said a word. Finally one arm was raised. It was Mooney.

"I'll go with ya Horace."

"Wait a minute Horace," said Palmer. "I'll write a note to Hightower in Hot Springs. It's not too far from here. He can get men together and join us in the morning. None of us are prepared to move forward now. Not even you and Mooney, Horace."

Since Mooney seemed to be free from any ill effects of the other men's ailments, Palmer asked him to carry the note to Sheriff Hightower. As Mooney wheeled his horse and headed for Hot Springs, Horace Poor and the others dismounted. Over the next couple of hours, most of them drifted off back to Aurora. A couple stayed with him to wait for Hightower's men.

∽∽∽

The stage to Los Angeles arrived on time. Mrs. Devine and other family members met Sarah at the station. They shared hugs and kisses. It was a wonderful reunion. They asked about the trip to Los Angeles. Mom wanted to know how Henry was. She inquired what Benton was like. Sarah answered all their questions. Then she told them all about Bob. It took nearly two hours.

# Gun Play at Convict Lake

## Stopping By at the McLaughlin Ranch

Jones roused his men early. He was getting excited. They were only two days out of Bishop Creek. He really looked forward to their arrival. He figured all the help he needed to get far away from any danger was right there. Sleepy, but equally anxious to get to their destination, the others did not put up any fuss about getting underway early. They had traveled along about three hours just off the Aurora - Owens River Toll Road. They were near Dobey Meadows.

Mary McLaughlin had been up since long before sunrise. James had ridden out just after sunrise to meet with others to round up a herd and bring it down to the winter range. She made sure her husband had a good supper packed for the long ride. She figured he would be back just after sundown. She loved her home. Here they were about two miles up Dobey Creek from Dobey Meadows. Fall was here. The Aspens were getting ready to show off with a display of bright orange and yellow.

Mary McLaughlin

James rode down the creek and beyond to meet with the others to drive cattle down for the winter. He thought of the long day ahead in the saddle. He did not even notice the men off the trail hiding in the willows as he rode by not 50 feet away.

"Wonder where he came from?" Questioned Lea."

Charlie replied, "Don't rightly know? Let's find out."

When James had passed some distance down the road, Jones and the others took the trail leading up along Dobey Creek. Even these hardened criminals saw the beauty of the foliage bordering the flowing water. They had traveled about two miles when they saw the McLaughlin Meadows Ranch. Mrs. McLaughlin was on the porch knocking the dirt out of her rugs. She saw some

## Gun Play at Convict Lake

riders and two men on foot coming up the road. It was not that unusual for travelers to come by from time to time. Somehow she sensed these men were a bit different. Born and bred a rancher's daughter, she knew the proper way to greet visitors.

"Morning."

"Morning ma'am," responded Lea Morton. "We're powerfully hungry. Would you have some grub to spare?"

"Sure do," she responded, due in part to her upbringing. "Tie you horses up over at the barn. I'll put a fresh pot of coffee on. You can dust off over there as well if you have a mind too."

Morton, Black, Jones and Burke dismounted. They tied their horses to the rail by the barn. Each took a turn at the water trough to wash off the dust and dirt. When they were done, Russell and Cockerell got a turn.

Charlie had checked the barn and the corral. He did not see any other mounts. He led the group to the house. Ever so politely he knocked on the door.

"Oh come on in. Coffee will be done in a minute. I've got flapjacks, eggs, potatoes and fresh sausage. Pick a spot at the table. Just relax and make yourself to home. I won't be a minute."

Morton's dinners were not bad, but Mary McLaughlin's breakfast was something special. Her cooking was top notch. The men could not believe their good luck. The food was delicious. The portions were mountainous.

"You boys get enough?"

"Yes ma'am," came a chorus from the men.

"Where you boys headin?"

"We've been promised some work near Independence,"

## Gun Play at Convict Lake

lied Charlie. "We hope to get there in about five days. We'd have been there already, but the boys have had some bad luck with horses. We lost two this week. When part of your party is on foot the goin is slow. This bad luck has cut in on our provisions too. We're pretty much out of everything."

"Well, my husband butchered out a steer a couple days ago. I can let you have a good supply of meat. Let's see. There's some extra salt, some coffee, some flour and a few extra potatoes. Will that help?"

"Sure enough," said Burke. "That would be great."

"No problem at all. We're blessed with plenty."

"Speaking of your husband," said Lea, "where is he?"

"Oh James is off helping to drive cattle to Adobe Meadows. Most were brought down out of the high country and are being moved down here for the winter. He'll be back tonight."

Mary had been gathering up supplies while she talked about James and what he was doing. She had placed what she had in a couple of large sacks.

"Well here ya go," she said, pointing to the sacks. "These items should help you get along way towards Independence without starving. Is there anything else I can do for you boys?"

"Well now that you mentioned it," smiled Lea, "there is. You see I've actually been in prison for the past several months. I haven't had the company of a lady in all that time. I would really like to spend a few minutes with you alone."

The blood rushed from Mary's face. She turned and ran to the bedroom, shutting the door behind her. Charlie looked at Lea and smiled.

"Ok Lea, I guess you're first. Don't be too long and don't mess up the goods. I like my ladies looking real nice."

"Don't worry Charlie, I'm a real ladies man."

"Come on boys," said Charlie, "wait outside. I'll see what I might find of use in here while I wait for Lea. He'll let us know when it's time for the next one."

Burke, Roberts and Cockerell looked on uncomfortably. They felt very bad for the lady. She had just done them all a good deed and now was being taken advantage of very unfairly. But

## Gun Play at Convict Lake

none of them had the courage to speak out to Morton or Jones. Black seemed to side with Charlie and Lea. They could tell from his eyes he could hardly wait his turn with her. While lingering outside in the living room, Roberts and Cockerell found some useful clothing. It included a warm coat, pants and a flannel shirt. Tilden put the coat on and gave the shirt to the boy. They could not help but hear the screaming coming from the bedroom.

✧✧✧

When James McLaughlin arrived home, he found his wife in a corner of their room in tears. Her clothes were disheveled. He reached down for her. She pulled him to her. She just wept in his arms uncontrollably for several minutes. She could not talk. The words just would not come out. James did not know what to think. Finally, she gathered herself enough to talk.

"Convicts, convicts," she sobbed. "They were here. They hurt me. I'm sorry. I'm so sorry."

James was speechless. He held Mary tightly and tried to comfort her. He was livid. He wanted to kill someone. He could see her tormentors had not beaten her, but they had obviously physically abused her.

"James," she said between tears. "You need to ride to Benton and get men to help you find them. Don't you try to get them yourself! I'll be all right. You need to go now. I'll be all right."

He picked her up and laid her on the bed. He covered her with warm blankets. He got her a glass of water and made her drink some. He looked for their bottle of whiskey. It was gone. He kissed her gently on the forehead.

"You take care, honey. I love you, Mary. You rest now. We'll get them. I promise."

He immediately set out for Benton. His instinct was to set out after them on his own. But that would be senseless. They would have him out gunned. He rode on as fast as his mount could carry him.

Had he known that Jones and party were camped just three miles west of his ranch, James might have been riding in a different direction. With the exception of Roberts, Burke and

## Gun Play at Convict Lake

Cockerell, the Jones gang thought their stay at the McLaughlin Ranch was, well, stimulating. Being the lowlife characters they were, they bragged about their afternoon exploits. The more of James' whiskey the three drank, the more descriptive they got.

"Tilden," said Burke in a hushed tone, "we've got to get free from this bunch. No good is going to come by staying. I don't care who Jones knows. This isn't going to end well."

"I agree. But we need to do so without causing a big fuss. Such a fuss could go bad for us. We'll just find a place and time to slip away from them."

&&&

Mooney finally made it to Benton Hot Springs. He inquired about the sheriff at the General Store and found he had gone home. He was directed to his residence. He knocked on the door. When Hightower opened it, he handed George the note.

"Well I'll be," quipped Hightower. "I'm sure we can get a posse together. Follow me back to town."

Hightower took Mooney with him back to the Store. It was after the dinner hour. Henry and Bob were sorting through freight that arrived during the afternoon. George walked right in.

"Listen up, there are six escaped convicts over near Adobe Meadows. Sheriff Palmer needs help in tracking them. Bob, please see who you can round up. I'm going to send Henry ahead as soon as he can go. I want you to ride with me in the morning."

"Okay George," said Henry. "I'll change and saddle up."

"I'll close up and gather up some men," said Bob.

Rapid hoof beats were heard coming down the grade toward Benton. James McLaughlin pulled up in front of the general store. Bob, Henry, Mooney and George were on the porch.

"James," said Bob, "what's wrong?"

"Convicts went through our place today. Mary treated them kindly. Before they left, they hurt her. I made her comfortable before riding here. She's going to be okay. I want to catch those bastards. They can't be too far away."

"Mooney here is from Aurora. He just brought us word of Sheriff Palmer and others close to your place. They were follow-

## Gun Play at Convict Lake

ing the convicts. We're getting a posse together now."

"Good," said James. "When do we leave."

"I'm sending Henry right now. Do you want to go too?"

"Yeah. Yeah I do."

"Okay Henry, I want you to ride all the way to the sawmill tonight. If you see them, just watch em. Don't confront em. The rest of us will be there soon. Don't get yourselves in trouble."

The two started toward the sawmill, arriving a little past 11. They did not see anyone on the way or when they got there. As much as James wanted to continue, Henry kept him in check. James decided he could wait till morning to take out his frustrations on those he despised so much. They bedded down. Henry quickly fell asleep. Not James. His mind was preoccupied.

As Morrison went through town trying to find others willing to go after the outlaws, Hightower walked back to his house. He wanted Martha to go out and help try to comfort Mary. But he did not want her going alone. Along the way he saw Clancy Wardlow. Clancy was a former lawman from Kansas.

"Clancy, there's been trouble at the McLaughlin's. Those escaped convicts went through there today. I would appreciate it if you'd take Martha out and stay the night. I don't expect any further trouble, but I'd feel much better if you're with them."

"I'll be happy to oblige, George."

"Thanks. Take my buggy at the shop. That big bay will get you there in no time. I'll go tell Martha she's takin a little trip."

∽∽∽

In the early morning light, James saw some movement at the sawmill. He walked over to see about a cup of coffee. Henry was still asleep. James told the man in the cook house about the posse expected this morning. The man figured someone would be coming. He had seen Charlie Jones late Wednesday right there at the sawmill. He had ridden right up, stepped off his horse and boldly asked for some provisions. The cook gave him some bread, meat and salt. Most of them knew Charlie from his days riding with Ben Clark. There also had heard he had broken out of prison at Carson City. They did not know much else.

# Gun Play at Convict Lake

## Benton Hot Springs Posse Hits the Trail

The Benton Hot Springs posse assembled at the sheriff's office at eight am. George sent them over to the local dining hall for breakfast. Bob rounded up eight others to join them. He had asked Mono Jim, an Indian tracker to accompany them. It was nearly nine when the men mounted up and left town.

Henry and James had an early breakfast at the cook house. James was ready to start the hunt at first light. It was now around 11. Henry used his good judgment to keep the man in check until the posse got there. Finally, a distant cloud of dust was seen.

"That must be them," Henry said.

"It's about time," exclaimed James.

Hightower led the posse into the sawmill yard. He saw James and Henry walking up. "Good morning James. I had Clancy drive Martha out to your place last night to look after Mary."

"Thanks. I'm sure she'll be glad to have Martha there."

Hightower had the men dismount. The group waited for the Aurora party. About two in the afternoon, Sheriff Palmer and Horace Pool arrived. They dismounted and tied up their horses.

"Afternoon George," said Palmer to Hightower. "Sorry we're so late."

"No problem, we're glad you made it."

"Oh, excuse my manners, this is Horace Poor. His brother is the mail rider that the convicts are holding hostage."

"Howdy, Horace," said Hightower.

Horace smiled in return. When James heard the comment about the mail rider hostage, he knew he needed to speak out.

"George, when Mary told me about these bastards, she never mentioned anyone being held hostage. I'm sure the mail rider wasn't with them. She would noticed something like that."

This was not what Horace wanted to hear. He had held onto the hope that these outlaws had his brother. Now it seems his

## Gun Play at Convict Lake

quest was in vain. He looked over to Palmer. "Sheriff, in light of this news, I'm heading back home. Maybe there is news there."

"I think I'm going to ride back home with ya. George and the boys can take up the chase from here. Good luck, boys."

With that, the weary duo swung around their mounts and headed down the trail towards Aurora.

"Gather up, men," said Hightower. "We're gonna ride back toward James' place to see if we can find their track."

About two miles up the canyon, Mono Jim found the convicts' trail. They followed it for about 18 miles across the Owen's River, near Benton Crossing and down into Long Valley. Mono Jim said they were close by. The posse moved ahead cautiously.

&&&

John Wheeler was glad to be close to home. His ride to the Armagosa Mines was long and hard. He looked forward to seeing Ludwig. He knew his partner would hold up his end of their plan. He figured he'd skirt the White Mountains until he found track of Ludwig and whoever else he had gathered together. He hoped that John had already found the trail of the escapees.

&&&

A dispatch was sent from Wellington station that stated the remains of William Poor had been brought in by the group tailing the convicts. He was killed about 15 miles in a southeasterly direction from Wellington. Poor was found about a half mile below Sulphur Springs, 200 yards west of the road. He was shot in the head and his body had been burnt. Naturally an outcry for the capture and hanging of the men responsible came forth.

&&&

Mono Jim, Hightower and Morrison were at the head of the group following the convicts' trail. They were encouraged that signs of the men were very fresh. Then all of a sudden, there they were, just ahead of them, in a cloud of dust. Bob Morrison was the first to see them. He immediately held up his arm. The posse stopped. The other members saw the dust. It was late afternoon

## Gun Play at Convict Lake

and nearly dark. It looked like they were heading into Monte Diablo Canyon. There was a stream and a good sized lake back there. There wasn't any outlet.

"Bob, I think it's better we wait until morning before we go in after them. Trying this in the dark is not a good idea."

"I agree. We can get some food and bed down at the McGee cattle camp just over that hill. Alney's bound to be there."

"Good idea"

"Men, we're gonna wait till morning. We'll ride to the McGee camp and see about some food. Follow me."

Hightower turned his horse and led his posse toward Alney McGee's cattle camp. Alney was a Owens Valley stockman who grazed his cattle in Long Valley to take advantage of the lush grass. It took about 30 minutes get there. They could see smoke coming from the line shack. It appeared someone heard them approaching. They stood on the porch watching.

"Howdy George, boys, what's all this?" Said Alney. "I'm sure you're not here to help me gather in the cows."

"Howdy Alney," said Hightower. "There's six convicts in Monte Diablo Canyon. In the morning, we going after them. Can we bed down here tonight?"

"Certainly! You know George, I heard something about a breakout at Carson City. Are these guys from there?"

"Yep, it's a small bunch of em. We think they killed a mail rider back near Sweetwater."

"Well, we don't have much here, but we always like company, no matter what the reason. I'll have the wife put another pot of coffee on and get some grub ready, too."

"Thanks, Alney."

"No problem. Oh, this is Han Gunter and that's Inman."

"Pleased to met ya, fellas."

Inman nodded and Han waved at George. The posse dismounted. Saddles, blankets and bridles were removed. Horses were turned out. Alney's wranglers threw some hay into the corral. Before long bed rolls were laid about. Firewood was gathered. It was going to get chilly outside over night. Alney himself cooked steaks. He made sure everyone got enough to eat. The

## Gun Play at Convict Lake

men knew what was ahead of them. One by one they settled back on their bedrolls. Morning would come quick enough.

Mrs. McGee was busy with her biscuits long before sun up. With the scent of bacon sizzling on the stove, it wasn't long before she had company. Steaming cups of coffee warmed them up. With full stomachs, the posse set about their chores. Guns were checked. Horses were saddled. Hightower's men were ready.

"Thanks for everything Alney," he said. "And you ma'am, you sure do know how to make a man want to get outta bed."

She smiled and watched as the sheriff rode down the trail. George knew it was a 30 minute ride to Monte Diablo Canyon.

"I sure would like to ride with them this morning," said Alney, "but we've got work to do."

"Well boss," Han commented, " I'm glad we have our regular chores to attend to. I never much cared for gunplay myself."

"I'm with Han," said Inman.

ಌಌಌ

John Wheeler decided to rest his horses before trying to locate Ludwig in the White Mountains. He was riding along, looking for signs of his partner. A familiar sight brought a smile to his face. He saw a small rock formation along the trail, a marking they had used for years to alert each other. This one told him to head up the trail into the Whites. John knew he could not be more than a couple hours behind his partner. He could see Ludwig had company. There were at least four other horsemen in the group.

ಌಌಌ

The Devine family was staying at the Pico House on North Main Street in Los Angeles. It had been built by Pio Pico, the former Mexican Governor of California. It was considered the finest hotel in the entire Southwest. Sarah thought the place was wonderful. It was ornately decorated. The rooms were comfortable and very tastefully furnished. The dining room was spacious. The food was varied, plentiful and delicious. Most of all she enjoyed the time she was spending with her family. She missed Bob ever so much. She wondered what he must be up to now.

Gun Play at Convict Lake

# The Deadly Shoot Out at Monte Diablo

It had been a quiet 30 minute ride back to the mouth of Monte Diablo Canyon. Each posse member knew this was dangerous business. They knew convicts had Henry rifles with them. They had a great respect for weapon. They knew the average man could shoot 15 shots with the Henry rifle in about 12 seconds. They had to be extremely cautious. Hightower had taken the lead since leaving McGee's place. He raised his arm to stop the men.

"Ok boys, from here on in we have to be very careful. I don't want anyone yelling out or doing anything foolish. We have them outnumbered. If we keep our heads together, we can get in, surround them and get out of here without any of us getting hurt. Any questions?"

There were none. Bob and Henry had been riding together. Naturally, they were looking out for one another. The men had formed a close bond. It had developed long before Sarah had come to Benton and changed Morrison's entire life. Soon the two men would be brothers.

"Hold up Henry, I got to share something with ya," said Morrison, "I have a real funny feeling about all this."

"What's that."

"Well, I just feel if I ride in that canyon, I'm not going to be coming out. That's a terrible feeling."

"Geeze Bob, if you're having those thoughts, perhaps it's better that you stay here and watch for anyone trying to get by."

"I can't do that. I feel it's my duty to help apprehend these bastards. I just have an uneasy feeling. I'm sure I'll be okay. It's just a really bad feeling."

"Hell, we're all a bit anxious. We'll be all right."

A quarter mile up Monte Diablo Canyon it was a calm, peaceful morning. The sun was out. Pristine Monte Diablo Lake [*Convict Lake today*] reflected the huge granite mountain [*mt. Laurel today*] that overlooked it. Fish

## Gun Play at Convict Lake

jumped at the flies skimming the water's surface. Morton was resting and Roberts was asleep in a clear spot among the willows. Black had gone up the hill for an early morning constitutional.

Charlie Jones had looked forward to his day with great anticipation. He was saddled up and raring to go. He tucked a pistol in his belt. He did not need one of the rifles. Today was the day he was going to find the help he knew was awaiting him. The other fools did not need to get involved. The hell with them. It would be a lot easier to get provisions and an outfit for one than for six. He had gotten them this far. From now on, they would be on their own. He swung aboard his saddle.

"Hey, listen up," he said. "I'll see you fellas late tonight or tomorrow. It's time I get into the valley and see what kind of help I can get us. Stay out of trouble until I get back. Tell Burke and Tilden to stay put, too. Hey, where are they anyway?"

"Roberts said they left about an hour ago to look for wild berries," replied Morton. "What do you care?"

"I don't. See ya later Lea."

With that he moved back up the trail they came in on the previous afternoon. He was happier right now than he had been for over two years. Nothing could wipe the huge smile off his face. But then something did! Ahead, not a 100 yards away, were

## Gun Play at Convict Lake

horsemen in a circle. They appeared to be listening to someone in the center. He immediately dismounted and quietly led his horse across the creek into a heavily wooded willow grove.

Burke and Cockerell were not out picking berries. They had decided this was the place they needed to make their break from Charlie and the rest. Acting like they had not care in the world, except hunger, the two left the willows camp, never to return. They had carefully worked their way up the steep hill south of the lake. Aside from the tin cup that was supposed to be used for berry collecting, they each had a pistol and some cooked meat. The men figured Charlie would just get them killed if they stayed with his bunch.

As they cleared some rocks high above the lake, they could not help but stop and take in the beauty of it all. As they did a 360 degree look at their surroundings, they suddenly saw a group of mounted men at the beginning of the canyon. The two immediately slunk down so no one could see them. As they watched, the body of men moved up the trail to the lake ahead. Surveying the scene they saw a figure working his way down the mountain above where they had made camp in the willows. As he moved, he knocked some rocks loose and they rolled down hill making a bit of noise in the process.

After giving his men their orders, Hightower had Mono Jim hold the horses of a couple men sent to prevent anyone from getting out along the creek. They headed up the trail toward the lake. About a hundred yards up the canyon there came a noise and a man was seen running down the hillside. Before Hightower could remind his men to be careful, one fool hollered out:

"There they are boys!"

The posse immediately spurred their horses. They did not know the outlaw's camp was just 40 feet away. They also did not notice the figure in the willows moving slowly in the opposite direction. While all the commotion was going on behind him, Jones managed to slip by Mono Jim and led his horse down the canyon and away from danger. Once clear he mounted up and rode as far and as fast as he could.

Morton was sleeping when he heard the posse member's

## Gun Play at Convict Lake

yell. He kicked at Roberts to wake him up. Together they retreated to a large tree and hid behind it. Unfortunately, neither of them had grabbed a weapon. Black, the figure running down the hill, hit the ground just a short distance above them.

"Roberts, go back there and grab those rifles."

"Are you crazy?"

"Get those rifles, boy or they're gonna kill us all."

Moving towards the weapons, Robert was hit by a shotgun blast, with pellets tearing into his lower leg and foot. He winced when hit and fell. Somehow he managed to crawl to the rifles. He retrieved the saddle bag with the cartridges and the two rifles. He moved to make his way back to the tree and caught another slug in process. It tore a hole in the fleshy part of his back. Morton and Black watched in amazement as the boy struggled to got back to them with the weapons. Roberts took cover behind a large pine tree with Morton. Grabbing a Henry, he yelled to the kid.

"Get back in the willows, they surround us here and I'll get shot!"

Obediently the wounded boy retreated to the willows. He lay there in pain from his injuries. Roberts was armed with a revolver, but was in no condition to fight. Morton tossed the second Henry up to Black. With a smile, Lea checked to see if his rifle was loaded. Black did likewise. As soon as Black and Morton opened fire on the posse, the fight was virtually over. In a matter

## Gun Play at Convict Lake

of seconds a hail of gunfire ripped through the willows surrounding the posse. Sheriff Hightower's horse was shot out from under him. "Oh my God," he thought as gunfire echoed off the canyon walls. Seeing it was futile to continue he yelled at his men.

"Stop. Fall back. Retreat."

He voice was barely audible over the roar of gunfire. Morrison heard him. As he turned, his horse was shot and they fell together to the ground. The terrible gun battle continued. It lasted for more than 20 minutes. While Morrison tried to work his way to cover, a hail of lead was directed his way. He felt a deep burning sensation in his side. He winced. He thought about what he had said to Henry not long ago. It hurt, but he had a mission. These men had to be stopped.

No one in the posse saw that Bob got shot. The posse members did not need Hightower's command to retreat. They found a safe haven. George was there.

"Damn," exclaimed one, "I've never seen anything like that. It's murder back in that canyon"

"Where's Bob," asked Henry. "Did any of you see Bob?"

"I saw him and his horse go down. He looked okay. He was trying to get to cover," said Hightower.

Meanwhile, Morrison was intent upon getting closer to those firing at him. He wanted a good shot at the convicts. Morton and Black watched his movements. They had fired so many rounds that the barrel of their rifles were too hot to hold. They waited for the man working his way toward them to offer them a better target. Black was watching him.

"There's a brave chap, I don't like to kill him."

"That's the kind to kill," remarked Morton. "Then you won't have any trouble with the cowards."

Black, armed with his six shooter, left his cover. He moved quietly while working to get around behind Morrison. He had lost sight of the man for a moment. Morrison was hiding in the brush. Someone was coming towards him. The man walked right by him. Bob had a perfect shot. He cocked his pistol and pulled the trigger. To his dismay, the weapon misfired. Black, startled by the noise, blindly turned and shot at Morrison. Bob was struck again.

## Gun Play at Convict Lake

Black saw his bullet hit him. He thought he had fatally wounded the man. He moved toward Morrison to retrieve the dead man's weapon. But, wounded and weak, Morrison attempted to raise his gun and fire at Black. Unfortunately, he lacked the strength. Black looked down at him. Bob saw the man standing before him. At point blank range, Black shot Morrison in the head. His premonition proved to be true.

During the gun battle, Burke and Cockerell fled right over the mountain they were climbing. It made no difference that there was not a trail to follow. They knew their lives depended upon getting as far away as possible. They did not stay to watch anything. But they did hear the roar of continuous gunfire echoing through the canyon. It was like a nightmare. The two men found some rocks in which to hide.

Charlie Jones heard the gunfire as well. He figured Morton and Black were pleased he did not take one of those Henrys with him. It sounded to him that they were making good use of them back there in the canyon. His timing could not have been more perfect. He figured Bishop Creek was but three or four hours away. Soon he would be among real friends. He would turn on his charm. Everything would be fine now.

Black and Morton knew they had the posse on the run. For the time being they were safe. Lea wanted to get out of this canyon. Roberts had been hiding in the willows during the battle. He managed to get to his feet. He hobbled over to Black and handed the man his gun.

"Moses, we've got to get outta here. Please help me. I can hardly even stand up by myself."

"Leave him," said Morton, "he's gonna die anyway. The kid's no good to us. Never has been. I'm sure somebody will be

## Gun Play at Convict Lake

along shortly to deal with em."

Black looked kinda sideways at Morton, but said nothing. The two men started working their way out of the canyon. They were well shielded by the willows. They moved about three hundred yards and then stopped. Roberts was trying his best to follow them. He had made a cane out of a willow branch to assist him in moving along.

Three horses were grazing in a meadow just ahead of Morton and Black. Lea watched as Moses easily walked up and caught them. He figured these animals came in with the posse. As they continued walking ahead leading the horses, they saw a figure standing in the willows several yards up the trail.

Mono Jim was standing on a nearby hillside. He was holding horses as instructed. He saw some men approaching and mistook Black and Morton for posse members. As the two approached him, Mono Jim shouted to them.

"There are three convicts down in the canyon without any weapons, go in and shoot them!"

Almost immediately, the Indian realized these were not posse members. He turned and ran into the willows to find shelter. He did not make it very far. He was shot by Black. As he fell he fired at the men. He missed the outlaws, but hit one of their horses instead. Morton raised his Henry, took steady aim and shot Mono Jim in the left eye. The Indian fell dead on the spot.

Morton walked over and took the reins of the Indian's horse. He swung aboard. It was rodeo time. The horse bucked, turned and dodged all at once. Morton was soon airborne. He hit the ground with a thud. Black could not help but let out a belly laugh. Morton stood up and dusted himself off. He walked toward the horse, pulled his pistol from his belt and shot it between the eyes. The poor horse buckled at the knees and went down.

Meanwhile, two members of the posse had been able to capture three horses. They mounted up and cautiously followed the outlaws. As they watched from a distance, they saw the exchange with Mono Jim. It sickened them. The men returned to the mouth of the canyon to give Hightower a report.

"George, they've killed Mono Jim. There's two of them

## Gun Play at Convict Lake

passing up and out of the canyon on that southern ridge. Anyone following them will be killed for sure."

"You're right," replied Hightower. "We need to get in the canyon and find Bob. I'm sure the outlaws have all cleared out of there by now."

Walking or on horseback, the posse followed Hightower and Devine to the scene of the fight. They moved very carefully. There was a chance a wounded outlaw remained and posed a threat. They crossed the creek and saw a body lying in the willows. Henry jumped off his horse and ran ahead. He saw his friend in a pool of blood. He fell to his knees. Others crowded around.

"Oh no. No. No. Oh Bob, what did you do?" Cried Henry. "Why didn't you just stay back with us. Oh my Gawd, what am I gonna tell Sarah?"

Henry completely broke down. He sobbed uncontrollably. Hightower tried to console him. It did not help. The other men wiped tears from their eyes. Morrison was a friend to one and all. James McLaughlin quietly took a bedroll off his saddle and laid it over his friend's body.

At the McGee cattle camp, Alney and his hand were busy as usual. There was always something that needed to be done. His wrangler had stopped a moment to wipe his brow. He saw dust along the ridge and realized that horsemen were coming down the hill at a run.

"Hey look there boss, there's a couple of riders makin good time. Lets get up there and see what's up."

"All right."

Off they started on foot at a trot. McGee was a true frontiersman. He had fought in the Indian wars and was no fool. He suddenly became suspicious.

"Hold up there. I think we better stay here. If they're bad news, we are stuck here unarmed."

Up on the ridge, Morton and Black saw two figures below them. They dismounted to see what they were up to. Lea had a great shot at the two from his current position. No doubt Alney's action saved his life as well as that of Han. Seeing the men stop, Morton and Black mounted up and continued on their way.

## Gun Play at Convict Lake

"I'm not sure what that was all about, but since the posse was here last night, I want to ride over to the canyon and see if they're okay."

They saddled up, buckled on their gun belts and took their rifles with them. It took them about 40 minutes to find Hightower and his men.

"George."

"Alney."

Alney McGee

"What's up here?"

"We got routed. Their Henrys took the fight away from us. We were just plain outgunned. They killed Morrison and our guide. I'm pretty sure they went up and over that rise."

"I'm sure they did. Han and I saw two riders moving along quickly. We started out to see who they were. When we did they stopped and dismounted. When Han and I stopped, they just rode off. I'm sure that was two of them. How many were there?"

"I was told there were six. But all we can account for are three. You said you saw two. Perhaps one is lying out there dead or dying. I sure hope so."

Alney was an old hand at dealing with tragedy. He asked a couple of the boys to bury Mono Jim. Morrison was wrapped up in the bedroll. His body was tied across a saddle. Alney led the horse back to his place. Most of the posse headed to McGee's place to recoup. McGee could tell these men were in shock.

# Gun Play at Convict Lake

## Morrison Buried - Morton and Black Hang

After their near encounter with McGee and his ranch hand, Morton and Black moved as far away from the scene of their murderous adventure as was possible. Along the way they had gathered up some potatoes and other vegetables. They stayed up high on the rim of the valley so they could see if they were being followed. So far as Morton could tell, no one was following them. He stopped his horse and dismounted.

"Moses, this is a good place to stop for the night. We've got a good view in all directions. If anyone comes after us, we'll see them first."

"Sounds good. Man that was something back there."

"That it was. I'm sure glad that Charlie didn't take a Henry with him. Our firepower kept us alive."

"Yeah, that plus that guy's gun misfired. Otherwise I'd be dead back there."

"Well, it just wasn't your time, that's all. I wonder if they found that whiney kid yet?"

Roberts had watched in horror as Morton and Black deserted him. He tried to follow, but was in too much pain. He lay quietly in the willows and watched as the posse members gathered up the dead man that Black shot. He feared they would fan out in the willows and find him. For whatever reason, they did not. He heard the sounds of a shovel at work. He figured someone was burying the man that Morton killed. Before long it was silent, save for the birds and the winds blowing through the leaves. Although unarmed and crippled, he had to find a way out of this canyon. He followed the trail left by Morton and Black, using the cane he made. The boy made 50 yards or so at a time. He looked for a spot to rest that afforded a break from the wind. He found such a place in a rock formation. There was tall grass nearby. He grabbed as much as he could to make himself a bed. The rest he

## Gun Play at Convict Lake

would use to cover himself to stave away the cold. He had nothing to eat and no water. The boy was miserable.

At the McGee camp, it was somber. Mrs. McGee had hot coffee for the men. Alney helped cook them up some supper. No one wanted to talk about the ordeal.

The following morning, the posse returned to Benton Hot Springs with Morrison's body. Six-year-old Ben Edwards had joined his father Thomas, a teamster, on a trip from Partzwick that day. It was a gruesome scene as young Ben stood next to his

dad and watched Morrison's blood spattered horse carry Bob's body along Main Street. It was unfortunate that Morrison's joking remark to Henry about being "buried in this suit" came to pass. Thus the love of Sarah Devine's life was laid to rest in the Benton Hot Springs cemetery with full Masonic honors. A large and grief stricken circle of friends attended the solemn ceremony.

When he arrived in Benton, Hightower had a letter sent by messenger to Bishop Creek. It told of the shoot out and requested help in locating the outlaws. Unfortunately, the letter did not arrive in a timely manner. Thus it was nearly 24 hours before local lawmen learned that help was needed. They quickly assembled a posse and started toward Long Valley. Hightower's communica-

## Gun Play at Convict Lake

tion had warned them about the Henry rifles. They picked up the outlaw tracks below McGee's camp. The men had circled around the place and headed south. They tracked Morton and Black up into Pine Canyon, a rough, rugged terrain that they knew gave no exit to the convicts. They pressed them so hard that the convicts had to shoot one tired horse and lost another over a precipice.

The posse decided it was crazy to go against these men armed as they were. A courier rode to Camp Independence to request arms and men to help them. Major Egbert and a detachment of five men were selected to help. They set out for Pine Canyon.

Sunday night, Roberts saw a light on the mountain side some distance away. He did not care who this was. It looked warm. After much suffering, he succeeded in crawling to it. Imagine his surprise when he found Morton and Black around the fire.

"Well I'll be damned," said Lea, "look what crawled in. How ya doin boy? There's some fellas down the hill there that would like us to surrender. Do you want to surrender?"

Roberts just shook his head. At present he was happy to be near a warm fire. He was disappointed to see the two did not have anything to eat. He was famished. He had not eaten in two days. He figured their position was such that anyone rushing them would be at the mercy of their superior gunfire. Exhausted and in pain, he fell into a comforting sleep. He was startled awake by the crack of a rifle just above him. He looked up to see Morton leaning against a rock, rifle in hand.

"I just wanted them to remember I'm thinking of em," he said, eyeing the boy. "They'll think twice about coming in after us. Hey Black, let's have Roberts work his way up that draw to see if we can retreat up there and get out of this mess."

"Send him on."

So, Roberts kept his head low as he maneuvered his crutch and body out of the fortification. He was blocked from view by the boulders. He made better time this morning than the previous evening. During his trek, he heard sporadic gun fire. It took him about an hour to make a half mile. He kept going. He really did not want to be around Morton. He knew the man hated him. Why he had not killed him already was a mystery to him. He decided

## Gun Play at Convict Lake

he could travel no further. He estimated he was about a mile and a half away. The gun fire had stopped. It was eerily silent.

During Robert's trip, Morton and Black were able to sneak out of their position and move back down toward Round Valley. The posse planned to wait until Yancy got back with help before trying to apprehend the men. Black and Morton were running for their very lives. They had managed to slowly get around the posse unnoticed. When they thought it was prudent, they began running for the river. They had traveled quite a distance, all the while looking behind them. As they expected, the lawmen finally saw they had out-foxed them and were now in pursuit.

"We've got to find a spot to make a stand," yelled Morton. "We'll hold them off until dark and try to move away again."

The two found a little rise that offered a pretty good view of the surrounding terrain. While watching the dust of the riders behind them, they rolled rocks to the rise to offer them better protection. It was not long before they had been penned down by the lawmen again. Down the hill, the posse fanned out and kept an eye open for a head to pop up. The range was over 300 yards. The chances of getting hit were pretty slim. One of the Indians accompanying the posse had been watching a figure rise and fire from the right of the rock formation. He carefully aimed his rifle about a foot above his expected target. There it was again. He fired. Black never felt the ball as it torn through his head. Morton saw him go down. He looked over and saw that nearly an eighth of his scull was missing from the back of his head.

"Moses," he yelled. "Moses, are you okay?"

To his amazement, he saw the man look up at him and nodded his head. "How can he do that with half his head gone," thought Morton. For the first time, Lea was scared. He never expected someone to put a bullet in either one of them from that distance. Finally he had enough.

"Hey," Morton yelled, "we surrender. We won't shoot anymore. Just promise us you'll take us back to Carson City."

"Throw out you guns," came the reply. "You're wanted in Carson City, that's were you'll go. So toss your weapons away and come out."

## Gun Play at Convict Lake

"Black's been shot. I'll have to help him out. It's no trick. Don't shoot."

Morton helped Black to his feet and they stepped around the fortification into the open. Several men scrambled up the mountain side to the convicts. Morton had his arms raised. Black stood there as if in a trance. They were taken to Bishop Creek.

Morton was interrogated. Black was not in any condition to talk. He said he shot the Indian. Morton pointed to Jones as the shooter in the mail rider's death. He tried the best he could to lay guilt on Roberts for other murderous deeds. Remembering how bad the boy looked the last time he saw him, he figured Roberts was dead by now. When asked where they might find him, Morton gave them a good lead. Two local lawmen, Hubbard and Nesmith, decided they would wait till morning to find Roberts.

Early Thursday morning Henry Hubbard and Hal Nesmith set out after Roberts. The men rode up Pine Canyon, past the rock fortification where the others had been. They found his track. He was easy to follow. They stopped for lunch, seating themselves by a spring to eat. They did not have much food with them.

"Maybe we should keep some of this for the kid, he's bound to be starved."

"Yeah, we'll keep a couple of biscuits for the boy."

While discussing the matter, they heard twigs snapping in the willows a short distance away. The noise was repeated. Heading cautiously toward the spot with guns drawn, they found Roberts. He was in considerable pain from the wounds in his shoulder and leg. They were badly infected. He looked half starved. When they helped him up he felt as though he was nearly frozen.

"Kill me if you must, but let me eat before you do."

The two biscuits they had left became but two mouthfuls for Roberts. The trio had a ten mile ride to the nearest house. Over and over on the way in, Roberts asked if there was anything else to eat. He was convinced there would be nothing at the house, but he was told there was plenty of grub where he was being taken.

Morton had spent the morning going over his account of their activities since the prison break. When Roberts was brought in, he turned pale. He knew the boy's story would be vastly differ-

## Gun Play at Convict Lake

ent from his. Lea had not figured the boy would be found alive.

Early Sunday evening, September 30, a light spring wagon rolled up front of the Bishop Creek jail. Morton, Black and Roberts were brought out and put aboard. A strong guard of horsemen was assigned to accompany the prisoners back to Carson City. The group started out. It was a pleasant evening. The stars were out and the sunset had left a faint red glow over the Sierra. About two miles out, they were surrounded by several well armed men.

"Who's the captain of the guard?" Said the group's leader, later identified as a Mr. Malory.

"I am," replied James Sherwin.

"Turn to the left and go on."

"I refuse to do so."

Suspense hung in the air. Morton looked up at the man. He looked at those guarding him. He sensed it was useless to argue.

"Give me the reins and I will follow you fellows, as I am a pretty good driver myself."

He was offered the reins. He took them and away he went, rapidly, to his own funeral. Roberts, who was lying in the wagon, protested. He had absolutely no choice in the matter. One of the armed men led the wagon. It wound its way across the valley. They ended up at a vacant house a mile or so away.

"You boys with the wagon, put your weapons over their in a stack. You'll get em back in a little while."

Black and Roberts, were carried into the house. Morton

## Gun Play at Convict Lake

looked around at the armed men. After a moment he stepped down off the wagon. He entered the house. Oil lamps were lit. A fire was built. A jury was organized. It consisted of all those present except for members of the guard. Roberts was put into an adjoining room. They asked him to make a statement concerning the prison break and events that followed up until the present time.

During the trial, jury members were allowed to ask questions. Morton tried to put as much blame on Roberts as he could. It did not work. The jury found Morton and Black guilty of the murders of Poor, Morrison and Mono Jim. The jurors were unanimous in their decision to have Black and Morton hang immediately. The decision on what to do with Roberts was not unanimous, so they decided to give Roberts back to the guard.

No tree was available, so supplies to build a gallows were sought. An old beam and some poles were found nearby. A scaffold was erected by placing one end of the long beam on the chimney. The other end was held up by quickly assembling a tripod from the three poles. Two ropes were thrown over the beam and secured tightly. A noose was fashioned on each. The wagon was driven under the beam. It would serve as the platform.

"Are you ready to die?" Morton asked Black.

"No, this isn't the crowd that will hang us."

"Yes it is. Don't you hear them building the scaffold?"

Black did not respond. Asked if he would like to stand nearer to the fire, Morton looked over to Roberts.

"It isn't worthwhile to warm myself now. We're to swing and I mean to have you hang with me if I can; I want company."

Black was carried out first and lifted to his fate in the wagon. Due to his head wound, he had to be raised to his feet, but once up, he stood stoically still without assistance. Morton walked out by himself and calmly surveyed the scene. Paying close attention to the cross beam and ropes he needed but little help to get into the wagon. As the noose was placed over his neck, he said:

"Take my coat, you don't want to put a rope outside a feller's collar. Please tie my hands more tightly, as I might try to grab the rope by instinct if they were loose."

"I would like some water," Black said.

## Gun Play at Convict Lake

"What do you want with water now?" laughed Morton.

Black was given a drink.

"Do you boys have anything to say," asked the hangmen.

"No," said Morton.

Black remained silent. They were asked if they wished to speak with a minister or have prayers offered.

"I told the minister everything I wanted to yesterday," replied Morton. "He said it wasn't well for a man to be taken off without some religious ceremony. If a minister would come I would like a prayer offered."

The minister took him by the hand, a few words were spoken and Morton who was facing the crowd said: "I'm prepared to meet my God. But I don't really know if there is any God."

Another short prayer was said which was only broken by a sigh once or twice by Black. As the word Amen was pronounced. The wagon was driven away from underneath the men. Black, being a large heavy man, died without a struggle. Morton, evidently to avoid suffering, sprung high off the wagon as it pulled away, most likely breaking his neck when the rope set. He died without a single movement of his muscles.

The armed citizens mounted up and left. Many of them were friends of Morrison. They felt justified. The guardsmen picked up their weapons. They helped Roberts back into the wagon. As they drove around the house he could see Morton and Black hanging from the beam. They took him to Bishop Creek.

Gun Play at Convict Lake

# Roberts, Burke and Cockerell Back in Jail

After Black and Morton were hung, Roberts was taken back to Bishop Creek. His wounds were so severe that the decision was made to transport him to Camp Independence so the U.S. Army Surgeon could properly treat him.

He had been wounded in the shoot out at Monte Diablo Lake in the left shoulder and left thigh, a little above the knee. Gangrene had set in before medical aid could be obtained. But the military surgeon felt he could save the leg and have Roberts traveling in about a month. Major Egbert agreed to keep the prisoner safely under lock and key.

Finally, Roberts was nursed back to good health. Hubbard and Neismith were dispatched from Bishop Creek to get Roberts and return him to Carson City. The three had an interesting trip back to the prison.

Near Benton Hot Springs, both lawmen had to draw their weapons in response to a crowd of 40 or more citizens that came out to hang Roberts. By sheer force and courage, the men drove the citizens away from the door of their room.

Sheriff Hightower arrived with a few men and helped the trio get out of town. Naturally, the young man was terrified as the mob was milling about the house where they were staying.

When they got close to Aurora, the men were more careful. Expecting trouble, Hubbard went ahead to check out the climate of the town. He found it very inhospitable. Upon returning to Roberts and Neismith, it was decided they would ride around Aurora.

Hubbard said Roberts prayed to be back in the Nevada State Prison. He was in constant fear of being hung along the trail. Hubbard was quote as saying that "if Roberts was given a horse he would had rode like the devil to the prison himself, just to find safety from hangmen."

## Gun Play at Convict Lake

≈≈≈

Wheeler finally found his friend Ludwig and Sheriff Helm. Together, they started into the White Mountains, where they spent nearly a week looking for signs.

Fresh tracks were discovered in Fish Lake Valley. John Ludwig guessed it was Burke. He knew that Burke was familiar with the region because Ludwig was tasked with taking Burke to prison after Burke was convicted of murder. Ludwig took Burke over this same route to Aurora.

Leaving Fish Lake Valley, Ludwig took the party up a canyon to an old ice house. They found a camp which appeared to have been quickly abandoned. Tracks were discovered that pointed up a rise.

It was here that the lawmen divided. Helm and another man went up one side of the peak. Ludwig and Wheeler took the other side. Some distance from the top of the peak Cockerell peeked over the rocky ledge. Ludwig pointed his Spencer rifle at the man's head. Cockerell threw up one hand, Ludwig kept a keen eye on the man and told Wheeler to demand that the convicts surrender. But suddenly, Cockerell disappeared. Ludwig dashed around the point, called out to Helm to look out for the convicts headed towards him. Then Cockerell appeared and walked toward his captors. Burke followed close after him.

They denied being with the Jones party or having anything to do with the mail rider's death. The men were taken to Aurora on their way to Carson City. At Aurora, two or three efforts were made to take the prisoners from the jail. The lawmen stood at ready all night to prevent a lawless action. Ludwig was offered $500 in gold to leave the jail unattended.

Gun Play at Convict Lake

# Whatever Happened to Charlie?

Where did Charlie Jones end up? Was he successful in finding help in Bishop Creek? Did he disappear into the Sierra, never to be heard from again?

This was perhaps one of the most discussed subjects surrounding the escape. Newspapers of the era put forth several possibilities as to what may have happened. That Jones' death was proved false on more than one occasion led one newspaper to remark about Charlie: "Like the wildcat at Piper's Opera House, he won't stay killed."

One story surfaced in October 1871 and was attributed to a gentleman who had arrived at Aurora. He stated that officers on the track of Jones and Burke, found Charlie's body. It was in an old cabin in the Fish Lake Valley. It was thought that Cockerell had joined Burke and Jones somewhere near Round Valley after the fight with the posse. The three slipped away together and headed to Fish Lake Valley. There they must have quarreled and Jones was killed. His body was not returned and no reward was ever paid for Jones. It seems logical that if this were true, Burke and Cockerell would have taken credit for killing Jones, who was held responsible with killing Pixley, Isaacs and the mail rider, Billy Poor. They never did.

A much more titillating account of how Charlie Jones ended up concerns an amazing shoot out with a Francis Armistead. This was published in several newspapers including the *Nevada State Journal*, December 30, 1871 and the *Coshocton Democrat* in Coshocton, Ohio, January 23, 1872.

According to the story, Armistead, who helped in the capture of Roberts, Morton and Black, continued on the trail of Jones. He followed Charlie's tracks about 50 miles from the head of Long Valley along the San Joaquin River. This may be the same escape route that Jones took after his fight with Mathews a few

## Gun Play at Convict Lake

years earlier. Armistead trailed Jones to a sheep camp in Visalia. Jones had stopped there for a couple days. Armistead introduced himself as a horse trader to Jones and the sheep rancher George Slawson. He said he needed to hire a crew help drive a herd of horses on to Arizona. Jones was excited about the job opportunity and hired on for the trip.

The three men all got along famously and Slawson cooked a wonderful meal. After dinner they all headed off to bed. In the morning Armistead took Slawson aside and told him who Jones was. He explained he planned to take him into custody for transport back to Carson City. Jones either overhead the conversation or just suspected Armistead was after him. In any case, he went into the Slawson ranch house and got a Henry rifle.

"I know what you're about," yelled Charlie as he stepped back out of the house, " you want to take me back to Nevada. I will die first."

With these words he leveled the rifle at Armistead and fired. The first round hit Armistead, who had a Henry as well. The fire was instantly returned. Jones was hit in the chest. A flurry of gun fire erupted. Both men fired round after round in the fight. According to Slawson, the men were but 30 steps apart. The hail of lead took its effect. From his eyewitness account, Slawson said Jones kept giving way with Armistead following him until Armistead fell to the ground. Jones rushed the fallen man. Armistead, though weak was able to fire his rifle and shot Jones in the head. This bullet killed him instantly. In all, Armistead reportedly fired fifteen shots. Jones was hit twelve times. The last shot was the fatal one. It was said that Jones fired eleven shots and that nine hit Armistead. Any one of those bullets would most likely have proved fatal after a time.

Slawson said Armistead hung on for about two hours after the gun battle. Slawson reported he was coolest man I every saw. He was perfectly calm. He said that if he had killed Jones, he was willing to die. His last words were "Tell her I love ..." Slawson understood he was speaking of his Aunt Sally. Before dying, Armistead made George Slawson promise to write down the account of this event and have it published. Apparently he did just that!

# Gun Play at Convict Lake

# Epilogue

The six escaped convicts that ended up at the head of Long Valley left a lasting impression on the geography of the region. As noted previously the Benton Hot Springs posse followed the outlaws into Monte Diablo Canyon. Nestled in the canyon was a spectacular Eastern Sierra Lake, from which a lively stream meandered its' way towards the Owen's River. These waterways also carried the prefix Monte Diablo.

It was not long after the deadly gun battle that residents of Inyo and Mono County felt compelled to rename the location. The lake at the site of the fight, once called Witsonapah by the Paiutes, along with the creek and canyon were named Convict Lake, Convict Creek and Convict Canyon.

To honor the sacrifice made by Robert Morrison, the brave Benton Hot Springs merchant that was killed by Moses Black, folks began referring to the towering 12,286 foot peak overlooking Convict as Mount Morrison. It is one of the most prominent peaks along the eastern front of the Sierra Nevada.

Years later, in 1987, a nearby mountain that reaches 10,669 feet, was named Mono Jim Peak, to honor the brave Paiute scout that led the Benton Hot Springs posse and was killed by Leandor Morton.

No further information was uncovered concerning Sarah Devine or her brother, Henry. Neither of their names are mentioned in the Mono or Inyo County census reports of 1880.

For a more detailed account of the 1871 Nevada State Prison escape, please read **Quest for Freedom**. It is available at your favorite bookstores or online at Talahi.com/store.

# Gun Play at Convict Lake

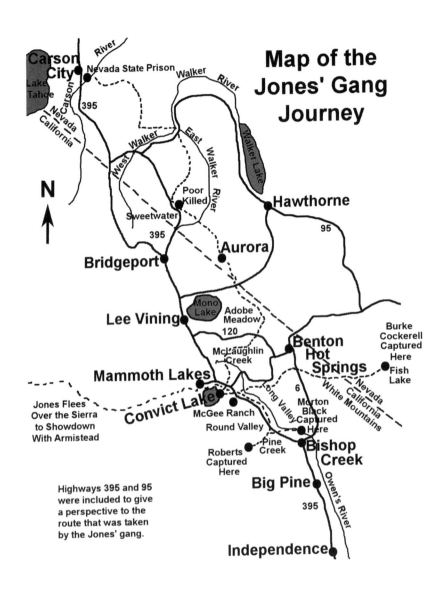